'It's obvious t
deception ru

Marcus spoke col

'You're despicable!' Alex replied.

'And you're forgetting something.'

'But I'm sure you'll tell me what it is.' She looked balefully at him.

'You happen to have entered into an agreement with me. Nothing has changed. Are you telling me that you intend backing out now that your little deception has been uncovered?'

Dear Reader

As Easter approaches, Mills & Boon are delighted to present you with an exciting selection of sixteen new titles. Why not take a trip to our Euromance locations— Switzerland or western Crete, where romance is celebrated in great style! Or maybe you'd care to dip into the story of a family feud or a rekindled love affair? Whatever tickles your fancy, you can always count on love being in the air with Mills & Boon!

The Editor

Alison York was born near Yorkshire's Moors and Dales but now lives in Warwickshire. A French graduate, she has two daughters and a son, all married, and two Siamese cats. She loves writing for the opportunity it offers to explore feelings and motivations. As well as novels, she writes short stories and poems. She is an avid reader—hell for her would have no books—and she also enjoys walking, gardening, theatre, music and art—other people's!

DEAR ENEMY

BY
ALISON YORK

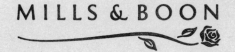

MILLS & BOON LIMITED
ETON HOUSE, 18-24 PARADISE ROAD
RICHMOND, SURREY TW9 1SR

*First published in Great Britain 1994
by Mills & Boon Limited*

© Alison York 1994

*Australian copyright 1994
Philippine copyright 1994
This edition 1994*

ISBN 0 263 78457 6

*Set in Times Roman 10 on 11 pt.
01-9404-59337 C*

Made and printed in Great Britain

CHAPTER ONE

THE girl rose suddenly from the screen of rushes that still hid the lower part of her body, her honey-toned flesh glistening from the fresh water of the stream that ran into the lake at that point.

The rider, who had approached silently over the soft lakeside ground, unheard and unseen, reined in his horse, watching her across the narrow arm of water that separated them. Ondine... he thought, with the shadow of a smile. But living Ondine, not the water-sprite of the legend. She was real, and all woman.

Beside her there was a dead tamarisk, its gnarled trunk and limbs emphasising the golden, rounded beauty of the girl's raised arms as she lifted her hair away from a touchingly vulnerable neck before letting it fall again. The sun was breaking through the early morning mists now and shining bright and brazen, striking answering fire from the cascade of rich, dark copper that fell luxuriantly on to the slender shoulders.

He had a momentary strong male urge to see the face framed by that vibrant hair, the curves the white bikini-top covered, the legs that would surely equal the shapeliness of those arms. But the urge was quickly disciplined. He had no desire to have this flesh-and-blood Ondine turn and see him in the role of voyeur. The moment should remain what it was—one of the Camargue's lasting images to take back home to Sussex with him. He turned his horse, then spurred it rapidly to a gallop, not caring now about the splash of its hoofs through the shallows.

*   *   *

5

Alex Leeward turned to look into the sun after him, seeking the cause of the sudden noise that had alerted her and shading her green eyes with a wet hand. An involuntary smile curved her lips as she saw the white jeans, white shirt, white horse with flying white mane and tail. The White Rider... she thought, unconsciously naming him as he had named her. His speed startled the flamingoes at the far end of the neck of water. They rose with raucous cries from their mud-pie nests, circled in agitation, then streamed off in the direction of the sea, necks stretched out, legs trailing, pink plumage unbelievably bright against the blue of the sky.

Their noisy departure in turn disturbed a group of wild horses which, up to then, had been peacefully grazing. They came splashing through the reedy shallows, gathering speed towards the girl until the spray from their passing showered over her. White, with the flying manes and tails of the White Rider's horse and wide, flaring nostrils, they were an unforgettable sight with their brown foals running between their flashing hoofs.

The rider, a small figure in the distance now, was almost out of sight. The one alien note in his dazzling gear, the black *gardian's* hat he was wearing, had slipped off to rest on his shoulders, and the girl saw the glint of gold from fair hair as he rose rhythmically in his saddle.

For a few brief moments he had been part of the magic of this wild place, part of something that enchanted her. But enough of fanciful dreaming. Someone who was stranded, penniless, her money and her return ticket to England stolen, should be dealing with practicalities, not flights of imagination.

She went purposefully back into the deserted *gardian's cabane* where she had spent a far from comfortable night. What she had to do now was finish getting dressed and then embark on the escape scheme that had been suggested to her last night when she was brought to the *cabane*. If the scheme was valid, she would be able to work her way back to England. If not, it was a case of back to the drawing board. She was definitely not going to phone home for help. Her parents had barely recovered from a trauma with one daughter and could well do without problems with the other. An embassy might help, though heaven only knew how far she would have to go before finding one. And how on earth would she get to it with not a franc to her name, not even the price of a modest coffee and croissant for today's breakfast?

An hour or so later, wearing jeans and a jade shirt, and carrying her soft case with a duffle-bag slung over her other shoulder, Alex was standing checking the board at the entrance to a *mas*, as she had learned to call the farm properties dotted around the Camargue. Yes—this was the one, the Mas de Malmont. And it was obviously into the tourist business in a big way, for the board announced that English, German and Spanish were spoken for the convenience of guests taking part in the horse-riding holidays in which the Mas specialised.

Immaculate white fencing bordered the drive she was about to turn into. Beyond the fencing, in the distance, Alex could see a group of black Camargue bulls, yearlings, she guessed from their size, corralled and most likely waiting to be branded. They were bellowing their unease and apprehension across the spiky saltwort. She shivered a little, sharing their unease as she walked.

She hoped she looked respectable. Everything had been a matter of guesswork since there had been no such thing as a mirror in the deserted *cabane*. She had brushed her jeans well, and her shirt was fresh. Her hair had been washed at the hotel where she had spent the previous night before disaster struck, and it was good-humoured enough to take care of itself after skilful cutting without the need of much fussing. In any case, there wasn't a thing she could do about her appearance, so she might as well get on with things and forget it.

Trees screened the property. She went through them and found herself in a central yard with the graceful farm building surrounding her on three sides. There was a sign indicating an office on the right. Alex put down her case and duffle-bag near the wall, and, feeling a ripple of apprehension, knocked on the door and went in.

The grey-haired French man with a healthy outdoor tan who was sitting at the desk looked up and enquired how he could help her. When she asked for, 'Monsieur Mark, *le visiteur anglais*,' as instructed by Liz, who had not known the man's surname, he got up and opened a window on the far side of the office away from the courtyard, and shouted in French that Alex had no difficulty in understanding.

'*Hé*, Mark! You've struck lucky! There's a pretty little redhead asking for you.'

Then, grinning at her, he excused himself and went off across the yard to enter the building opposite by a door in the far corner, leaving Alex alone with her apprehension.

The place was very quiet, and the stables across the courtyard were standing empty, their doors wide open. A bronzed, leathery-looking man in traditional blue overalls was mucking out at a leisurely pace. The holiday riders must have left early on their daily trek. Nervously, now that she was so near either salvation or drawing a blank, Alex occupied her mind by counting the pots of flowering geraniums along the wall opposite, then the panes of glass in the office windows. Any futile thing to keep herself calm. At last she heard footsteps approaching and the door of the office began to open.

Someone spoke, and whoever was opening the door stepped back into the yard to answer something that the worker in the stables opposite had said to him, coming into view from the window. Alex was able to get a good look at his back view and saw gleaming fair hair curling low into a suntanned neck. He put up a hand to run his fingers through it, and there was the same glint of gold sunning over a bronzed well-muscled arm. Disbelievingly she realised that her eyes were moving slowly down over a dazzlingly white shirt tucked into the trim waist of white jeans. In this land of Mediterranean dark heads and olive skins, it was improbable that there could be two men with this colouring, and both of them addicted to dressing in white. With the unreal feeling of stepping into the fantasy world of fables, she realised that she was looking at the White Rider. She was sure of it. And she could feel the knowledge setting her pulse racing and the palms of her hands growing damp as her green eyes widened, unable to tear themselves away from him.

Then he turned, and from the leafy screen of a weeping fig plant through which she was looking she saw his face for the first time and the imminent encounter switched from the realms of the fabulous to those of the darkest nightmare.

She knew him! God, how she knew him! Not from the earlier encounter, which had hardly been an encounter at all, but from a much closer and infinitely more shocking and world-shattering family involvement. It was as well that the stable hand detained him again, for she couldn't have spoken, so petrified were the muscles of her throat with the shock of the sight of him.

He was the man who had jilted her sister Elaine, who had split their family life at the seams and come perilously close to removing her father from it permanently, for the pain and shock of what happened to Elaine had brought on a devastating coronary from which John Leeward was lucky to have made a heart-breakingly slow recovery.

The man she was here to ask a favour of was a Wakeford, and the Wakefords and the Leewards had cut off all social contact two generations back. Indeed, it was because he had discovered that Elaine belonged to the hated Leewards that this man had dropped Alex's sister like a red-hot coal. Alex had never actually met him, but she had seen his photograph. Elaine had shown it to her and sworn her to secrecy, half full of bravado, half terrified of the family reaction to her budding relationship with the least eligible man in the world from the Leeward viewpoint.

He moved towards the door again, and the paralysis that had rooted Alex to the spot dissolved in a wave of hot fear. She crouched down and pretended to be occupied with the lace of her trainer, desperate to put off the face-to-face encounter. She had seen enough to know that he had not changed much. On a purely physical plane there was the same glossy sweep of loosely waving fair hair, bleached even fairer now by the sun of Provence. There was a power in the regular features that lifted them beyond the realm of the merely handsome, a firmness in the jawline and a squaring of the chin that made a very positive statement about personality. He looked every inch a man who knew what he wanted and where he was going. That he also knew what and who he didn't want Alex's sister had found to her cost. It was the eyes that said most about him. Grey, assessing windows of a soul that it was wiser not to look into.

Alex wanted to be wrong. If she blinked slowly, would she look up and see a different face in front of her? Someone who looked like a Wakeford, but turned out only to have a superficial likeness? She willed for it to be so. She saw his feet in burnished riding boots enter her field of vision and knew that she could put off the moment no longer.

He spoke, and it seemed wrong that his voice should be deep and one that if she had not known who he was she would have thought pleasant.

'The Lady of the Lake, I believe!'

'Sorry?' She rose to her feet slowly, unconsciously brushing back the bright hair that had betrayed her as surely as his had betrayed him, pretending bewilderment at the mode of address.

He walked round to the desk. 'I saw you bathing in the stream earlier this morning. You can hardly claim not to have seen me after the racket the flamingoes made.' The grey eyes were cutting through her pretence with the cold certainty of steel. 'I take it your reluctance to own up to remembering the incident stems from the fact that you had a free night in the *cabane*? Well, you're certainly not the first to take advantage of the Malmonts in that way, and I don't suppose you'll be the last. In any case, there's no need to think up an excuse. It's no real business of mine.'

Alex seized on the present like a lifeline. It was so much safer than the past.

She swallowed and spoke more steadily than she would have believed possible. 'I did spend the night there. Only one night, and there was a good reason for it. I left the place exactly as I found it. It wasn't locked.'

'As I said, it's no business of mine.' His deep voice was calm, impersonal, dissociating himself from her peccadillo with a fraction of the uncaring ease with which he had severed his relationship with Elaine.

He sat on the edge of the desk, his undisguised scrutiny of her making her feel uncomfortable. His eyes, now that he had lowered himself on to the desk, were level with hers. Her mind raced, trying to find some magic answer to the question of what she should do. What could she *bear* to do was more like it. She was fairly sure that there was no reason for him to recognise her as Elaine's sister. She and Elaine were not at all alike in feature, and her own copper hair was far removed from Elaine's dark brown bob. Probably he didn't even know that Elaine had a sister. But as sure as Eve gave Adam the apple, he wouldn't want to have anything to do with her if he did know who she was. It would be far too undesirable and distasteful for him. So if she could bear in her turn to use him, somehow she must tread her way carefully around that one.

'Well?' he prompted. 'You asked for me by name, I understand. So what can I do for you? More to the point—what makes you think I *can* do anything for you?'

The problems of negotiating a return to England with not a franc to her name reared again in her mind. Alex swallowed, and took the plunge. If she could pull it off, she would use him and discard him, and that might have a bitter satisfaction of its own, drop him as he had dropped Elaine. There would be a certain flawed justice in that.

'I understand you're travelling back to England with a couple of Camargue horses?' she said.

The surprisingly dark eyebrows rose a fraction. 'Correct.' And what business is it of yours? the grey eyes seemed to be conveying, but he wasn't going to help her to stumble through what she had to say.

'I—I heard that you might be needing someone to give you a hand with them on the journey...with feeding and stabling and exercising. That sort of thing.'

'You were wrongly informed, I'm afraid. All the arrangements were made some days ago. There's no job going, if that's what you have in mind.' His reflective gaze rested on her. 'Someone's been having you on, it seems. Who was it?'

'Liz—when she showed me where the *cabane* was last night.'

Now she had his interest. He stood up, a frown furrowing his forehead. 'Then you've seen Liz since I have. Perhaps you can give me some indication of where she is? She was supposed to be around early this morning to see to the horses. I've had no rider for the second one.'

Being in possession of knowledge that she could divulge as opposed to the weight of the past that must remain shrouded in secrecy gave Alex's confidence a kick-start.

'When I last saw her,' she said with malicious casualness, 'she was on the back of her boyfriend's motorbike, heading for Saintes-Maries-de-la-Mer.'

'She was *what*?' His voice was dangerously quiet but his meaning crystal-clear. Someone—in this case, Liz—had not put his interests before all else. He glanced quickly at the Rolex on his wrist. 'Did she by any chance pause long enough to say when she intended to be back from this unscheduled little trip?'

Alex's green eyes met his. This was the crunch.

'I don't think she will be back. In fact, I know she won't. That's why I'm here. She told me you were going to need help.'

The grey eyes were icy now. 'Are you telling me that she's walked out on the arrangement we had?'

'Not exactly. She's just...changed it a little.'

'The devil she has!' He took a couple of impatient steps towards the window, then rounded on Alex, so that it took all her self-control for her not to flinch. 'And who talked her into it? You?'

'Certainly not,' Alex said with spirit. 'She may have suddenly realised that staying on in the Camargue was a possibility, once she knew that I was available to take her place. I don't dispute that. But the desire to stay on was already there. She has this French boyfriend, and things were getting rather serious with him. She really wanted to spend more time with him, you see.'

'On the contrary, I most certainly do not see,' he said, his voice chilling. 'The only thing that I see at the present moment is that Liz had contracted to travel back with me, doing absolutely essential work. And now, without a word of explanation, she has disappeared off the face of the earth. I have this old-fashioned belief—which no

doubt kids like you are light-years away from compre-
hending—that promises are meant to be kept, not
broken. And if there's to be a change of plan, I certainly
don't expect to be informed of it by a complete stranger
who has nothing whatsoever to do with the situation.'

Talk of keeping promises was rich, coming from him,
Alex thought fiercely. His own promises to Elaine had
broken under the weight of nothing more sinister than
a name.

And who was he to talk of her as a 'kid'? Who did
he think he was? Methusalah?

Before she could open her mouth and fall into a trap
of her own anger's creating, he rounded on her again.

'Who the hell are you, in any case? Why should I take
your word that this is really what has happened?'

When he had known Elaine, Alex's own name,
Alexandra, had been shortened to Sandie, a left-over
from schooldays. Alex should be safe enough.

'Alex.' She had a flash of inspiration. 'Alex Ward.'
The shortened surname balanced the abbreviated
Christian name he now sported himself. Elaine had
always referred to him as Marcus Wakeford. If he could
choose to be plain Mark, then she could be the equally
curtailed Alex Ward. The name was far enough removed
from Sandie Leeward to put him off the scent, if by some
remote chance Elaine had happened to refer to her. 'And
as far as taking my word for anything is concerned,' she
went on with quiet dignity, 'that won't be necessary. Liz
told me that she had left a letter of explanation in her
bedroom here. She anticipated your reaction.'

'My entirely normal reaction,' he said curtly. He made
quickly for the door, pausing only to say. 'Wait here,
please. I intend to find out if we are talking about a
situation that really exists before wasting any more time.'

When he had left the office, the shock of who he was
hit Alex with full force. She could do without all this
hassle, she thought fervently. It was bad enough to be

marooned here, but not bad enough, maybe, to make
her fight through this man's hostility—and not only his.
Her own for him was equally strong. And what would
she get for waiting? The extremely doubtful privilege of
spending days with a Wakeford—not just any Wakeford
at that, but the very one whose treatment of Elaine meant
that he had more stacked up against him than the whole
of the rest of his family put together. Their crimes against
the Leewards were shrouded in the mists of history as
far as Alex was concerned, but his were within recent
memory, and only too well documented. She had only
to look at her father's face to see them staring at her in
the strain left by his illness.

She made an instant decision and left the office.
Picking up her case and bag, she walked hurriedly
through the trees and headed off at a spanking pace down
the drive, her copper hair bouncing and streaming behind
her. Let the man find himself as much in the soup as
she was. Let him start from square one to sort out his
problems as she was going to have to do with hers. She
wanted none of him, and the same applied to the Range
Rover Liz had said he drove, and to his horses, which
she hoped he would have the devil's own job getting back
to England. How yuppily pretentious to come all the
way down to the South of France to buy a couple of
horses, anyway. Surely there were enough perfectly good
horses in England. How like a Wakeford to make life
difficult—for himself as much as for other people.

She hadn't reached anywhere near the main road when
the Range Rover of her thoughts sped past her and
stopped with a scream of tyres, slewing untidily across
the dusty surface of the drive in front of her. Mark
Wakeford stepped down.

'Yet another female who changes her mind as frequently as her underwear, are you?'

'Having second thoughts is my privilege,' she replied,
her voice steady.

He read her intention and moved to one side to block her attempt to pass him.

'Might I ask where you are thinking of going?'

'Away from here,' Alex said simply. 'That, again, is my privilege.'

'Forgive me if I find that surprising. As recently as five minutes ago you were very much interested in doing the precise opposite.'

'That was then. This is now.'

They glared at each other until he breathed out impatiently. 'Don't you think this is all rather childish? I would have thought Liz's irresponsible behaviour might have given you the urge to show that some women are capable of behaving sensibly——'

'Back in the office I was classed as a kid,' Alex interrupted caustically. 'Thanks for the promotion.'

He went on, ignoring her, 'I hadn't finished with you. You put a proposition to me which I had neither accepted nor rejected. You could have done me the courtesy of waiting for my answer.'

'It isn't always wise to leap into the unknown with a proposition. I have firm ideas about what I don't choose to subject myself to, and I'm afraid that your attitude comes under that heading.' Alex faced him squarely, green eyes flashing.

'Typical redhead!' he sneered. 'A temper to match your hair.'

Alex picked up the case which she had put down. 'I came here in good faith, thinking that I could save you trouble and step into the gap Liz left. You changed my mind for me. There's nothing more to be said.'

He reached out, took the case from her and put it firmly down on the ground again. 'I think there is. Calm down and listen to me. Let's not be stupid enough to burn bridges before we see whether it might be possible to cross them to our mutual convenience. You gave me a rather unpleasant surprise with your revelation about Liz. Perhaps I reacted a little strongly.'

'Put rather more simply, I expect that means you've had time to realise that it could be far more difficult than you thought to find someone to help you with the horses,' Alex said sceptically.

'Interpret it any way you like. Something tells me that your willingness to step into someone else's shoes means that your desire to get back to England by this means is as strong as my need for help with the horses.'

Alex shrugged. 'Maybe. But not at any price.'

He gave a brief nod. 'So perhaps we would both be wiser to take time to reconsider.' He turned and opened the Range Rover's passenger door, and somehow, although she hadn't really meant to do any such thing, she found herself getting in while her bag and case were stowed in the back.

Perhaps her departure had been a little hot-headed, she persuaded herself as Mark Wakeford drove on to the main road so that he could turn full circle and head back down the drive towards the farm. There was no doubt that if she could get over her reservations about being involved, however briefly, with him, he could be very useful to her. And she was equally sure that she could perform the job Liz had been scheduled to do every bit as efficiently as Liz would have done it.

This time he drove straight round to the back of the farmhouse, and when they got out of the Range Rover he showed her to a table under a pergola heavy with bougainvillia and waved her into a seat.

'If I go and organise some coffee, do you think you can suppress the urge to run away again?' he asked.

'I can't very well run anywhere, can I? You've locked my luggage in your car.'

He gave a brief smile in a way that revealed he was perfectly aware of what he had done, and why he had done it.

'So I have. How observant of you. Coffee, then. I won't be long.'

He went into the house. Alex tried to convince herself that she was not being some kind of crazy fool even to contemplate travelling with this man. Nothing was arranged, she told herself. They were going to talk about it, that was all. She watched the bulls in the distance as they were thrown and branded, glad that she couldn't see in detail exactly what was going on. It looked a violent business. She had the uneasy feeling that there was symbolism in it, but she didn't want to think exactly how.

'Here we are.' He put a tray down on the table in front of her. 'I take mine black, with two sugars.' Pouring coffee was evidently women's work.

Alex saw to the coffee, putting milk in hers, her mouth watering as she saw that there was a dish of *petits pains au chocolat*. The first coffee of the day did its bit to soften her attitude, the *petit pain* into which she bit doing a little more.

'I must say,' Mark Wakeford said reflectively, looking at her over the gold rim of his green cup, 'I find it hard to understand why Liz should have agreed to help me get the horses back to England one minute and hared off with this French Lothario the next.'

'It wasn't a sudden whim. It was more a coming together of circumstances. She said she had grown very fond of François over the past few days, and once she knew that I was willing to take her place—that I had a very good reason for needing to do so, in fact—it all slotted into place.'

'She might have had the courtesy to tell me personally what she was up to.'

'I think she felt you might try to dissuade her.'

'She was right.' He put his cup down, refusing the refill she offered. 'However, we're stuck with what she's done now. So let's get down to business. Whoever comes with me needs to know what she's doing. Before you get too enthusiastic about filling the gap, let me tell you what's involved.'

'Liz told me, actually.'

'Nevertheless, I shall tell you again. The idea is to take the journey through France as steadily as possible, driving no more than three or four hours a day and giving the horses a good break and plenty of exercise. I can see it taking at least three days to reach the Channel coast, perhaps more.' He went methodically through all the details Liz had already listed, concluding with the blunt warning, 'It isn't going to be a picnic. I don't know how the horses will react to travelling, so I'm not booking ahead. It may be a case of sleeping rough wherever the night stop happens to be.' He gave her an assessing glance.

'That isn't something that would worry me,' she said levelly, then, as she saw his expression change to one she couldn't fathom, she added, 'Is there something wrong with that?'

'I was merely thinking that both you and Liz seem prone to make rather sudden, thoughtless decisions. She hares off into the blue on the spur of the moment with someone I don't think she knows very well. You profess yourself ready to spend upwards of three days—*and nights*——' he placed emphasis on the 'and nights' before going on '—with a man you know even less. One can't help feeling that in today's world you should both know better.'

Alex looked him straight in the eye. 'I know myself. That's good enough for me.'

He held her gaze for a moment, then shrugged.

'No point in debating minor issues for the moment. So—what's the good reason you referred to? The one that makes you so keen to take Liz's place?'

She thought he had missed what she had said on that score. But apparently he missed nothing. She felt such a fool of circumstance, but she had to tell him.

'I had all my money stolen at the festival in Saintes-Maries-de-la-Mer. All my money, my travellers' cheques, and my return ticket. I'd met Liz and her friends earlier in the day and stayed with them to watch the gypsies' procession. There were masses of people down by the sea to see the statues carried into the water, and when I discovered that my wallet was missing I knew at once that it was going to be impossible to find whoever had taken it. Liz and co took me to the police station, and even bought me dinner afterwards. The rest—well, you know what happened next.'

'Oh, yes,' he said drily. 'And I know exactly what you expect to happen now. Your motives are crystal-clear. You expect that I shall conveniently step into the role of timely provider of meal ticket and travel warrant.'

'In return for services rendered,' she retorted quickly. 'I presume Liz wasn't doing three or more days' work for nothing. It ought to be worth a passenger fare across the Channel.'

He gave her a scornful look. 'Don't worry. If you're hired, you'll be paid. *If.*'

'Apart from necessary expenses, I wouldn't touch a penny,' she said emphatically.

'Is that so? And I suppose if you got your hands on a knife you'd cut that pert little nose off to spite your face.'

'Please don't be patronising,' Alex said stiffly.

'You take things very seriously.'

'Only as seriously as they are meant.'

He pushed his cup across the table. 'I'll have that second coffee now.'

With heightened colour Alex refilled their cups. Was she wasting her time? Damn fate for putting her in this position. Why couldn't it have been an absolute stranger taking horses back to England—someone with no painful, unpleasant echoes from the past? They drank their coffee in silence broken only by the distant bellowing of the yearlings. Me too, she thought with feeling.

'Of course, if you can't handle a horse, you'll be no good to me,' Mark Wakeford said at last.

'I'm not afraid to put my ability to the test. I've ridden all my life.'

'But these horses haven't *been* ridden all theirs. They're comparatively newly broken. And they're Camargue horses. I don't want anything adverse to happen to either of them on the way back.'

'Any more than I should want anything adverse to happen to me,' Alex said crisply.

'That too, I suppose.' There was no doubt what the order of rank was in his opinion.

'So this is what I propose,' he went on. 'You stay on here for the rest of today, during which time I shall satisfy myself as to your competence as a rider. If I'm satisfied, we set off as I had planned tomorrow. How does that strike you?'

'It sounds fair enough,' Alex said grudgingly.

'Then let's get on with it. You'd better come and meet Henriette Malmont. She'll let you use the room Liz had——' he gave her a direct look as he rose '—so whatever happens you'll get a more comfortable night than the last one. And, if nothing comes of today's trial, at least you'll have a little more time to find whatever other solution to your problems may prove necessary.'

Alex stood, looking defiantly at him. 'I shall cope.'

His mouth twisted sardonically. 'I don't doubt it. One of today's women...ready for anything, however unwisely.'

He turned on his heel and she followed him into the house, her eyes on the taut white shirt stretched over his broad shoulders, thinking how little he knew what truth he had just spoken. She was a mass of conflicting torments. Was it really worth throwing herself into this potential volcano of bad feelings, just to get a lift home? Could she bring herself to be civil to this man who had so much to answer for as far as her family was concerned?

She was going to have to be a damned good actress if she was to see it through, because the last thing on earth that Marcus Wakeford must find out if she did manage to bring herself to work for him was that he was actually doing a favour for—and, perhaps even worse from his point of view, having a favour done by— a Leeward.

CHAPTER TWO

HENRIETTE MALMONT, a plump, dark-haired, un-flappable-looking woman, was busy doing what looked like a dozen different jobs at once in the kitchen. She listened to the account of Liz's departure, her only re-action being a smile, a philosophical shrug, and the comment, 'She's young! You must expect anything of the young, then nothing surprises. *Voilà!*' Alex was very welcome to take over Liz's room, she said. One little moment, and she would be taken to it.

Mark Wakeford, having arranged things to his satis-faction, which gave Alex's lip a strong desire to curl, left them, saying that he would bring the luggage up to her room later. When she had completed the two huge *tartes aux pommes* that she was in the throes of filling with neatly overlapping slices of apple, Henriette took Alex through the typically Provençal long dining-room with its huge table capable of seating at least thirty people, and led her out into the corner of the courtyard. There, they turned into a concealed staircase leading to the rooms over the stables. At the top of the stairs, bed-linen was collected from a cupboard, and Alex was asked if she would mind making up her own bed.

'I'm happy to do anything to help,' Alex told her thankfully. 'It's so good of you to let me have the room.'

'One goes, one comes—it's the way of life here,' Henriette said simply. Then, with a few instructions about the whereabouts of the bathroom and laundry-room, she excused herself and hurried back to her kitchen.

Alex looked thankfully round her quarters for the night. What a change for the better from the *cabane*. Her room was one of half a dozen or so opening off the corridor. It had a cool, tiled floor, cork-coloured, the inevitable and necessary shutters at the window, and pleasant, simple pine furniture.

She stripped the bed and remade it with the bright cotton bedlinen she had been given. When she had taken the dirty linen along to the end of the corridor, she came back and leaned on the sill of her open window, staring down into the deserted courtyard. Marcus Wakeford appeared, startling her into drawing back slightly. He was carrying two lots of tack, and as she looked down on his gleaming head and easy stride Alex acknowledged the ripple of something that was far removed from hostility running through her. Grudgingly she admitted to herself that she could understand just why Elaine had become so involved with him. Even knowing his actions and the consequences of them, Alex could still see that he was the sort of man who drew even the least susceptible woman's eye and set the imagination of the more vulnerable of the sex smouldering.

He dropped the tack at a stable door, and looked round, first in one direction, then in the other. Alex realised that he was conscious of being watched, and, disgusted with herself for being fool enough to react to his undeniable physical attraction, she moved hurriedly away from the window before he looked up and saw her, and sat on the bed. She had no doubts about her ability to handle a horse, but handling a Wakeford, and especially this particular Wakeford, was a different matter entirely.

Meeting Marcus—or Mark as he seemed to call himself now—had brought back all the anxiety she had felt on Elaine's behalf two years ago. She couldn't help reliving that time now, all that had happened painfully vivid in her mind.

Alex had been in her last year of training as a physiotherapist, and she had only begun to find out about the
potential disaster waiting to happen in her sister's life
when she came home for the Easter holidays.

With one failed teenage marriage behind her, Elaine's
emotional life was a matter of prudent concern for all
her family. It was obvious from the moment that Alex
saw Elaine on the Wednesday before Easter that her sister
was in a highly charged mood, and it soon became perfectly clear that a new boyfriend was the stimulating
factor. But Alex was puzzled by the vague way Elaine
referred to him. It was uncharacteristic.

'Important, is he?' she asked.

'He could develop into something really serious. In
fact, I'm not sure that he already hasn't done just that.'
Elaine sounded as though she meant it, but, again, she
gave no concrete information.

'Then how come we don't get to see him?' Alex asked
bluntly. 'You don't usually draw this kind of discreet
veil over your love-life.'

'Ah, but this is different.' Elaine looked hesitantly at
her sister, then seemed to make up her mind. 'If I can't
tell you, who can I tell? I'll show you a photograph that
nobody else has seen.'

They were in Elaine's bedroom at the time, and Alex
was intrigued to see that the photograph was taken from
beneath the lining paper of the bottom drawer in the
dressing-table. Elaine passed over the photograph almost
with reverence. Alex looked at the face of the man in
it. At first she was relieved. Not only was he undeniably
worth looking at, there was a strength and firmness about
the face that reassured.

'Well, lucky old you!' she said. 'He's gorgeous. No
wonder you keep him to yourself! What's his name?
Adonis?'

There was no laugh from Elaine. Her answer was utterly serious.

'Do you swear not to tell anyone until I say it's safe to do so? If you don't, I'm telling you nothing.'

'Come on, Ellie! I'll swear anything you like to know just what the big mystery is.'

'I'm serious,' Elaine warned.

'So am I. I won't breathe a word to a soul. Now come on! Give!'

'Prepare yourself for a shock, then. His name is Marcus.' Her eyes held Alex's. 'Marcus Wakeford.'

Alex's voice came out as a squawk. '*Wakeford*! One of *the* Wakefords? You've actually fallen for a Wakeford? Oh...my goodness! That'll certainly put the cat among the pigeons as far as the parents are concerned.'

'Never mind the parents,' Elaine said ruefully. 'First I've got to tell Marcus that he's been going out with a Leeward for the past couple of months.'

'You mean he doesn't know?' Alex's heart sank. It was turning into another of Elaine's foolishnesses. She looked at her sister's timidly defiant face with a mixture of love and despair. 'Of course. Your name wouldn't mean a thing, would it?' She sank down on to the bed. Elaine had married almost straight from the schoolroom, and taken less than a year to repent at leisure. She was now divorced, but still used her married name, largely because she was in the same job that she had first taken as Elaine Vickers.

Alex's green eyes met the worried blue ones of her sister.

'Oh, Elaine! You've got yourself into a pretty heavy situation, haven't you?'

Elaine pulled a tragic face. 'I know. At first it was all a bit of a private laugh, but now I don't feel like laughing any more. I'm going to tell him, truly. But in my own time, and without any interference from family until I've sorted things out with Marcus. I don't give a tuppenny damn for the fact that he's a Wakeford. As you said, he's gorgeous. And not only that—he's such a terrific person. Really, really nice. I just know it'll be all right.'

Alex didn't care any more than Elaine did about the family feud. Two generations back a Wakeford had by devious means prevented their grandfather Leeward's marriage—a marriage arranged for both love and land— and snatched the intended bride with her territorial dowry for himself. In those days it had been a life and death matter. Their grandfather had lost the land, but he had not rested until he won back the woman. It was the briefest of victories, though. The unhappiness of a moral scandal in those days and the unrelenting attempt of Francis Wakeford to reclaim his wife had resulted in the distraught woman's suicide. Both men were fierce in their sense of wrong, and no reconciliation between the families in that generation could be dreamed of. Alex understood that. She and Elaine, when they had talked about the matter, had even conceded that seeing the Wakefords prosper with their ill-gotten land while the Leewards made a very modest living could make their father bitter about what might have been his. But it seemed to have little to do with them. Their grandfather had eventually married again, and happily. They and their father had resulted from that marriage. Grandfather Leeward had died before they were born, so they had known none of the injured parties. Surely it was time to let the whole sorry business sink into oblivion? In any case, the Wakeford family had moved away from the little West Sussex town where both families had lived for generations, so the heat had of necessity gone out of the situation to some extent. But letting sleeping dogs lie was a different matter from lying with them.

'I know we think it's all in the past, but the thing is...can you count on Marcus feeling as relaxed about the situation as we do?' Alex asked her sister.

Elaine's answer was almost confident. 'I'm pretty sure he will. I think we're both too far into the affair for anything else to matter...' Her eyes sparkled wickedly. Elaine never remained down for long. One of the reasons she was always getting into trouble was that she seemed incapable of remembering how easily the last disaster had come about. 'I must say, Sandie,' she said, giving Alex the strongest of desires to shake the nonsense out of her, 'it certainly adds a bit of an extra thrill to things, this "forbidden territory" business.'

'Just don't play with fire for so long that you end up getting your fingers burned,' Alex told her worriedly, and rather prophetically as it turned out.

It took Elaine weeks to come clean to Marcus, and when she at last did the end result was, as Alex had feared, disaster. She had not foreseen the extent of it, though.

The first Alex knew of it was when she got a distressed phone call from her sister the night before she was due to come home after finishing her final exams at the hospital. Elaine told her that she was at the airport, on the point of taking a stand-by flight to America.

It was all over between her and Marcus. Her voice was broken, tight with stress and smothered tears. She didn't want to talk about it. She had been a fool. She was not at all proud of herself. All she wanted was to get away. She would write—but not to talk about what had happened between herself and Marcus. She just wanted to forget that. It was finished with, and she wanted no questions from anyone. What she wanted was a new life. She'd made a pretty rotten job of the old one so far.

Before Alex could break into the agitated flow of words from her sister, she heard a background announcement over the airport Tannoy, and with a quick, 'My plane—must be off,' Elaine was gone.

It had been left to Alex, she found when she arrived home, to explain the situation to her parents. Mrs Leeward, distressed and mystified by her elder daughter's hasty flight from home and country, listened to Alex's account and responded with distraught sympathy.

'Oh, my poor Elaine! The foolish girl! She must have been devastated to find that stupid business still had so much power after all these years. I couldn't understand why there had been so much reticence about the current boyfriend, but you know how it's been since that disastrous first marriage of Ellie's. We've all tiptoed around afraid, treading on eggshells. How on earth shall we tell your father? Oh, Sandie!'

'Suppose this Wakeford man hadn't cared about the old quarrel... How would you and Daddy have felt?' It was a useless question now, but Alex felt compelled to ask it.

Her mother's eyes, dark with distress, looked into hers. 'It was never my quarrel in any case. I just married into it. But I can't honestly believe that your father sets much store by it these days. If this Marcus had been a good man, I'm sure he would have accepted him. I know I would.' Her sweet face convulsed with grief. 'As it is, I'd rather like to kill him.'

'He's obviously no good at all.' Alex's words were bitter. She loved her foolish sister. 'He's turned out to be as hostile and prejudiced as any Wakeford has ever been.'

Mrs Leeward had been right to dread telling her husband. An outburst of bitter rage against the Wakefords was followed by a night made horrific by the coronary he suffered in the early hours. He recovered, but only just, and was forced into early retirement for which he was less than well-prepared financially. The old family home of three generations of Leewards had to be sold, and now Elaine and Alex's parents lived in a small house on an estate, about which they didn't complain, but the girls knew that the best that could be said was that they tolerated it. The old life had gone.

It was a year before the family saw Elaine again, by which time, as they had learned from her letters and phone calls, she was engaged to an American whom she brought over to meet the family. It was therefore inappropriate to make any attempt to rake up the past, and doubly so in the light of Mr Leeward's health. Against all the odds, they were delighted to find that Elaine seemed at last to have found the right man, both in her own opinion and in theirs. Now, two years later, she was happily married, and her first child, a boy named after her father, was the apple of the family's eye.

Marcus Wakeford's name had never been mentioned again, but in Alex's memory he remained the man who had changed the course of her sister's life, putting the Atlantic Ocean between her and her family, and almost ended the life of their father. She hated him. The old quarrel had taken on new life.

A knock on her bedroom door roused her, and when she opened it the *éminence grise* of her thoughts was there, holding out her two bags.

'Thanks,' she said curtly, her mind still seething with memories.

'Just a moment——' He stopped her closing the door on him. 'I want to speak to you.'

Grudgingly Alex opened the door a little wider, but didn't invite him into her room. The past was too strongly with her.

'Yes?'

'I've made arrangements for the rest of the day. We'll take a couple of horses out, and you can have ample opportunity to show what you can do.' He looked her objectively up and down. 'You'll be all right in those things. I expect we can borrow a hat for you.'

'No need to do that,' Alex said crisply. 'I have one with me. And I'd prefer to get into a pair of jodhpurs. I've got those as well.'

'Very convenient. You borrowed them from Liz, I suppose.'

'No. They're my own. The first part of my holiday was spent riding in the Vercors.'

He conceded nothing. 'Sounds promising—but you've still got to convince me. Come on down as quickly as you can.' He turned and strode off down the corridor. Feeling ruffled, Alex shut the door and fished her stretch jodhpurs out from the bottom of her bag.

They were the most cruelly honest of garments on anyone with bulges to hide, but on Alex's slender curves they only served as an enhancement. She changed the green shirt for a stone-coloured cotton sweater, pinned back her richly coloured hair with a tortoiseshell slide at the nape of her neck, pulled on her short boots, and headed down to the yard, her riding hat swinging from her hand.

Right, Mr Doubting Wakeford, she thought. Don't think you're going to have fun at my expense.

The two horses in the yard, held by a young boy who was talking to the grey-haired man Alex had seen in the office, were a surprise. One was a bay, and huge, the other, a little smaller, was a piebald.

Mark came out of one of the stables and walked across to join the men, and the eyes of all of them turned on Alex as she approached, the two Frenchmen looking at her with obvious pleasure, Mark Wakeford's expression less readable.

Alex indicated the horses. 'What's this? I thought you had bought a couple of Camargues.'

'I have. And you'll only ride those if you prove to me that you can ride these,' he answered smoothly. 'I told you that my horses were fairly newly broken, remember, and in any case Camargues are different. André here has kindly agreed to lend us two of his excellent trekking horses. Zizi is yours——' he slapped the piebald's rump '—and Pépin's mine. They're well used to the kind of riding we'll be doing today.' The last comment was made with a significant look at the other two men, whose broad grins hinted at some kind of in-joke. Alex ignored it, and concentrated on making friends with Zizi, who seemed amiable enough.

'*Vous désirez monter, mademoiselle*?' André Malmont held out joined hands. Alex put a foot in them and sprang lightly into Zizi's saddle, where she paused to fix her hat before walking the horse to the other end of the yard. There, she adjusted the stirrups. Her legs were obviously longer than the last rider's. Then she came back to the watching group.

'So far, so good,' Mark said, vaulting easily into Pépin's saddle and patting the nut-brown neck. 'Now— let's see what you can really do. *A toute à l'heure*, André.'

'Amuse yourselves well,' the owner of the Mas said in careful English, again with that 'I know something you don't know' smile.

Mark rode level with Alex, and she saw that he was wearing the black *gardian's* hat again.

'That won't be much protection if you come off,' she said, caught looking at him.

'I don't come off.' It was said quietly, but with supreme male confidence. They were coming round the left-hand side of the farm now, and entering a long, narrow enclosure. He urged his horse into a trot and called to her, 'Just do what I do.'

Alex followed him, turning as he did at the far end of the field and following him back over the stretch of rough ground. After the second turn, he stepped up the pace to a gallop, so that for the next two lengths of the field they were travelling through the cloud of dust raised by their horses' hoofs.

At the next turn, instead of slackening pace, he increased it and took the fence without warning. Alex followed suit, Zizi soaring easily over the bars, and when Mark called over his shoulder in mocking tones, 'Still up?' she pointedly used his own words of only moments ago in reply,

'I don't come off.'

She dug her heels into Zizi's sides, urging the horse to pass him, but he caught the rein and with a commanding, 'No need to show off,' slowed them down to a steady walking pace again.

'Well, I can see you're out of L-plates,' he said laconically.

'I told you I could ride.' Alex was still smarting from the fence, which she thought had been unfair and even potentially dangerous of him.

He glanced sideways at her and read her expression.

'If the jump's niggling you, forget it. Zizi could do it in her sleep. We haven't come anywhere near the unexpected yet.'

'Then I shall just sit back and expect the unexpected,' she told him coolly.

They went past the branding corral. The branding was over and the yearlings released to go and hide in their usual haunts, but the smell of burning hide and hair was still in the air, making Zizi and Pépin twitch their ears and whicker softly.

'This riding holiday of yours...' Mark Wakeford said suddenly. 'Were you alone?'

'No. With friends.'

'Did you lose them as well as your money? That does sound like carelessness.'

She glanced at his mocking face. 'No. I didn't lose anyone. They had less holiday than I did. I stayed on for a few days to see the Camargue. Does that clear up that little point?'

'Very reassuringly. Was it worth it, the staying on? This place isn't everyone's cup of tea.'

'I think it's wonderful.'

'In spite of everything?'

'In spite of everything. This morning when the flamingoes took off and sent the horses galloping past me—
well, what can you say about a sight like that?'

'I saw them, remember.'

'It was unforgettable.'

'You're speaking to the converted.'

She shot a quick look at him, a little startled by what
had almost been a normal conversation. He sat astride
his horse in his white gear like some goodie from a
Western. He was looking at her from under the forward-
tilted brim of his hat, and the summer-bleached fairness
of his hair was dazzling in the sunlight. He looked so
sure of himself . . . so much one of life's favoured ones.

'Obviously,' she replied drily. 'It's a heck of a way to
come shopping, otherwise.'

The grey eyes were veiled. 'Ah, but there's a certain
lady in my family who has very persuasive ways. She
saw the film *Crin Blanc*—you know it?—and nothing
else would do for her but a Camargue horse.'

'She was fortunate to have a husband who could
pander to her desires,' Alex said.

He gave her a strange kind of look. 'The young lady
in question—Rebecca—is only seven. Not, of course,
that I would deny any wife of mine the pleasure of riding
one of the Camargues if she wished.'

Alex was doing sums. The only answer her mental
arithmetic could come up with was that he must have
married someone who already had a daughter. Or have
been involved with someone before Elaine came on the
scene, and gone back to her with the belated intention
of doing the right thing by his own daughter. Whichever
was the case, for a seven-year-old to make such demands
and have this man travel the length of France to fulfil
them, she had to be a very spoiled brat indeed.

'You're a highly indulgent father,' she said, her voice
tight with disapproval. Then she reminded herself that,
no matter what had happened, Elaine was now perfectly

happy. She had better remember that and not let her resentment and critical faculties get out of hand. She had to get on with this man on the surface if she was going to travel with him.

They had reached the main road where they approached a horse-box parked under the trees. They stopped at it, and Alex stated the obvious.

'For us?'

'Good guess.'

'But it's not yours?'

'The one I brought over? No. Mine's the towing variety. This belongs to the Mas.'

She dismounted as he had done and took Pépin's reins while he opened up the back of the box.

'Since we could easily ride back to the Mas, I take it we're going on somewhere else,' she probed.

'Right again.' He glanced mockingly at her. 'You didn't think that was it, did you?'

She shrugged. 'I'm in your hands. So where are we going?'

'Patience. You'll find out eventually.' He jumped down from the box. Zizi's ears had flattened. 'Let's get her in first. Keep Pépin back for a moment.'

Zizi was coaxed in and rewarded with a hay bag. Pépin followed calmly and got his travelling rations too. Mark fastened the box, then he and Alex got in the front.

'Is it far?' she asked with studied innocence.

'Not very... But we want the horses nice and fresh for this afternoon.' He paused. 'And they'll probably be glad of the box at the end of the day,' he added maddeningly, implying much but giving little away.

Alex made a mental vow to give him the satisfaction of fobbing off not one question more, and it was quite a while before he broke the silence as they drove along the flat roads.

'Tell me, what do you do with yourself when you're not getting into tricky situations abroad?'

Apparently it was fine for him to do the questioning. 'I'm a physio,' she said briefly.

'A physiotherapist? I'd never have guessed.'

'There's no reason why you should. We don't get tattooed with our job specification.'

His grey eyes rested on her briefly. 'Such a very physical occupation. A hands-on business. You don't strike me as being the type who would find that easy.'

'How can you possibly know? It's little more than an hour since we met.'

'I'm rarely wrong about the kind of vibes people give out.'

Alex's heartbeat quickened in alarm. Her hostility was getting through to him. She was not being careful enough. She forced a smile.

'Maybe this is a first. In any case, physiotherapy is my work, and I enjoy it. Perhaps you have no experience of what it entails.'

'Only a brief encounter with a sports coach. Which is in a different class from submitting oneself to the attentions of a redhead.' There was a pause while Alex studiously ignored what he had said. 'Now you're thinking that that was far too sexist a remark for your taste,' he observed calmly.

'Well, wasn't it?'

'Factual, I thought. But then, I'm not as keyed up on these issues as you women are.'

'That's probably because you don't find yourself the butt of them,' she retorted.

They had left the main Arles road now, passing a signpost which Alex was not quick enough to read, so she still had no idea where they were going. But suddenly, as they rounded a bend in the road where there was higher scrubby vegetation than the average, she saw that there was a crowd of people in a vast field ahead, and seconds later Mark drove off into it and drew the horse-box up in line with a host of others.

At the far end of the field there were bulls, roped off—
a black mass of them, milling around. People on foot
and on horseback were thronging everywhere, and Alex
realised as she jumped down that there was a mouthwatering smell of barbecued meat in the air.

'I think we'll get ourselves something to eat first. The
horses will be happy enough with their hay bags,' Mark
said. 'Hungry?'

Alex was ravenous, but conscious of the fact that she
had no money. 'Not really. You go ahead,' she said
casually.

He looked hard at her. 'I expect to provide you with
food, you know, if that answer comes from misplaced
pride.'

'You have no idea how maddening this situation is for
me,' Alex said passionately.

'Oh, yes, I have. I'm looking at you.' His tone became
more bracing. 'Oh, don't be so ridiculous. You're practically drooling, I can tell. And you're going to need all
your strength this afternoon.'

The oblique, taunting remark was the last straw.

'If you really feel like doing me a favour, you could
let these hints that something dreadful's coming up rest,'
she said. 'You're going to have to tell me what's on the
cards sooner or later. I can wait until then.'

'But it's killing you, isn't it?' He gave a cool smile,
then took her arm and began to steer her through the
crowds. 'Come on. They don't believe in queuing in these
parts. Just act very determined.'

They collected delicious-looking kebabs and fragrant
ribs of lamb, cartons of salad, a crusty 'flute' and a bottle
of red wine, and finally some golden peaches before
working their way back to the horses. Mark opened up
the box and put a folded horse rug on the flap. They
spread out their picnic lunch, and got to work on it.

The bouquet of the wine was intense from its standing
in the hot sun. The meat had been marinaded in a magic

blend of herbs and oils, and there were succulent local olives in the salad. Alex gave herself up to the seduction of a feast of flavours.

'All right?' Mark queried.

'Perfect. Thank you very much.'

I'm actually having a picnic with this Wakeford man and managing to keep a civil tongue in my head, she marvelled. There was so much to see around them that talking was not really necessary, and the pleasure of the food and sunshine more than made up for the undesirable identity of her companion. She was sufficiently mellow when he gathered up the bottle and glasses to return them, to manage to say again, 'Thanks, Mark,' quite civilly.

'Actually, it's Marcus,' he told her, and the name, reinforcing his identity, gave her a stupid jolt. 'I cut it short over here because, much though I like the Malmonts, I can't stand what they do to my name. '*Mahhrcewse*,' he said, with wicked and what she supposed was fairly accurate imitation. 'And before you say it,' he went on, 'I know I murder their language too, but their version of my name makes me feel an utter fool. They, and everyone else, can cope perfectly well with the abbreviated version. We'll get the horses out when I come back. It's almost time.' With a significant look to irritate her, he launched into the crowd.

Alex watched his fair head, higher than those surrounding him, her eyes seeming reluctant to leave his progress through the crowds. Several of the women he passed, whose dark eyes also followed him, evidently were prey to the same problem.

She got up impatiently and made for the toilet tent. When she returned, Marcus was bringing Pépin out. Zizi was already hitched to a hook on the side of the box.

'I wondered if you'd done a runner,' he said over his shoulder.

'I'm hardly in a position to do that, am I?'

'That implies that you would if you could. Feeling apprehensive?'

'Interested, actually,' she said coolly.

'In that case, I'll give you some information. You're about to take part in an *abrivado*. Know what that is?'

'No. But I'd put any money on the chance of our black friends at the end of the field being involved in it.'

'And you'd be right. You're about to learn what it's like to have the job of taking them from one place to another. All you have to do is keep up with the rest of the riders, as close as you can, and go with the crowd. You won't have the option of doing anything else, really. But there's nothing to worry about. Zizi's done this many times before. Just concentrate on keeping on top of her, in every sense. If you're game, I think it's time we were off. Want a hand up?'

Alex refused his offer and unhitched Zizi before mounting unaided. Bulls! She wasn't going to let him see it, but she felt apprehensive to say the least.

As though at some hidden signal, the crowds were sorting themselves out to pre-arranged positions—people on foot to the edge of the field, riders to the centre. There was an air of excitement that was almost tangible.

A group of Camargue *gardians* in distinctive dress and carrying the customary trident were heading off up the field to where the bulls moved restlessly.

'They're going to pick out the animals they want. We don't get involved at this stage,' Marcus said.

Somehow, the *gardians* had separated seven or eight bulls from the herd, and the fence was being replaced to keep the rest safely penned. The riders formed a tight ring round the beasts, herding them down the field, and as they neared the waiting horsemen one by one the riders wheeled and joined in until a tight pack was surrounding the central core of bulls.

Alex and Marcus were swept up and along with the rest, and the pounding pack gathered speed as they

circled the field twice to the cheers and catcalls of the
onlookers. Then the gate into the road, closed for the
start of the *abrivado*, was flung open and the tightly
packed riders and their charges streamed out along the
road, heading heaven only knew where.

Alex's hair flew out like a copper pennant as she
crouched low over Zizi, her riding hat forgotten in the
strange excitement of the occasion. She found herself
uttering the same wild cries as the surrounding riders.
It was primitive, savage, wonderful!

She and Marcus were towards the end of the pack as
they entered the streets of a village. The thunder of hoofs
and the bellowing of the bulls and shouts of the riders
were amplified by the thick stone walls of the houses,
and soon cries from onlookers crowded into doorways
and windows added to the pandemonium.

Suddenly a group of youths burst out from an alleyway and flung a volley of missiles into the riders.
Something hit Zizi on the cheek, exploding in a cloud
of white, and she reared in alarm while Alex fought to
control her and hang on. She might have managed it
too, but for the fact that a motorbike started up in the
alleyway, and someone revved its engine to capacity.

Zizi reared again, whinnying and flailing wildly in the
air with her forelegs, in danger of overbalancing. Alex
took the only course of action and let herself slide over
the horse's rump to the ground. She landed with a jarring
thud to the bottom of her back, but she was up in a
split-second, snatching at Zizi's reins and directing a
stream of abuse over her shoulder at the boys. They were
actually laughing at her, and the heat of the moment
brought out her English and completely annihilated
her French, but her meaning was clear enough. She
achieved nothing, though. They merely went on laughing
in her face.

Marcus had been carried forward with the force of the charge, but he had wheeled round and was back with her almost as soon as she was up on her feet.

'Are you hurt?' He jumped down, and for a moment looked slightly concerned. Only slightly, though, and not for long. His shirt was clinging to his chest and his forehead was filmed with sweat. The *gardian's* hat was hanging by its thongs down his back. Even as Alex turned her anger on him, she had the mortification of a flash of recognition of his rugged male attractiveness. Then, as quickly as his concern, it was gone, and she was feeling as angry with him as with the yobs who had brought her off her horse.

'Not hurt—furious!' she stormed, waving her free arm towards the spectators. 'Those louts threw something at us. Look at Zizi—she's covered in white stuff. Morons!' she shouted over her shoulder.

To her increased fury, Marcus merely grinned in their direction and gave a dismissive wave of his hand.

'*C'est la première fois pour mademoiselle*,' he called, and his tone was almost appeasing.

'What difference does the first time make?' she snarled at him, brushing Zizi's neck and raising white clouds that made her cough. 'Flour! That's what it is. Savages!'

Marcus turned to her firmly. 'Stop that. You don't know what you're talking about. Are you scared to get up on Zizi again, or what?'

She was up and glaring down at him almost before he had finished the sentence. He vaulted easily into Pépin's saddle.

'Come on, then. I expect we've missed the end of this particular run, but we may as well see our own finish through.'

That was it, then, Alex thought bitterly, angry now on her own behalf as well as Zizi's. She had come off her horse. He would think her unfit to take care of one of his precious Camargues if she couldn't cope with a well-schooled horse. She was just wasting time from now on, hanging around with him—but what could she do about it? She glared daggers at his back as she galloped down the street after him until they began to meet the other riders making their way back for a second run.

Marcus did not turn his horse, confirming Alex's opinion that she had been written off for the journey back to England. Instead he dismounted and attached Pépin's reins to a rail in front of a high wall. Miserably, Alex did likewise. Then she realised that they were outside a bull ring.

'I'm having nothing to do with bull fighting,' she said emphatically. 'I think it's barbaric, and I totally disapprove.'

'Calm down, hot-head,' Marcus told her steadily. 'You're in the Camargue, land of long-lived, cherished bulls. Come over and have a reviver after your unfortunate experience, and I'll explain.'

They threaded through the groups of people who were making for the bull ring and found a café in a nearby square, where Marcus left her sitting at a pavement table under the trees and made for the counter without asking Alex what she wanted. I shall just refuse to drink, if I don't like what he brings, she told herself mulishly. But when he returned he was closely followed by the waiter, who put two misted glasses of fresh lemon juice, cold and delicious, on the table. Perfect, Alex thought grudgingly, and about the only thing that was perfect right now.

'Now,' Marcus said, 'let me tell you about the bag of flour.'

'Don't bother. I know I came off. No need to rub it in,' Alex said.

'I've no intention of rubbing anything in. I saw what happened. I was there, remember? But don't go on holding it against the lads you were berating. They were only doing exactly what they are supposed to do at an *abrivado.*'

'They were *what*?' Alex said incredulously.

'The general idea is that spectators do their level best to break the circle of riders and engineer the escape of a bull. They use any means whatsoever—noise, harmless missiles, personal confrontation if they're foolhardy enough. It was only a paper bag of flour, Alex. No big deal. Zizi was surprised, that's all. Not hurt.'

And what about my behind? Alex was thinking hotly. *That* was jolly well hurt. And she'd have a bruise to show for it tomorrow, too.

'Why on earth didn't you warn me, then?' she asked coldly. 'Wasn't that rather an omission?' 'Rather an omission' showed tremendous self-discipline. 'Bloody moronic' was what she was saying inside her head.

'Not at all. I wanted to see how you would handle the unexpected,' he told her smoothly. 'Warning you would have prevented that chance, but it wouldn't have ruled out some kind of surprise. You couldn't have foreseen the exact incident. Zizi would still have been triggered off.'

'Well, now you've seen how I handle the unexpected,' Alex said bitterly.

'So I have.' He sipped his lemon juice. 'And now let me tell you about the next event.'

With an effort she tore her mind away from her terrible disappointment and followed what he was saying.

There would be no swords, no blood deliberately shed in the bull ring. The aim of the contest between man and beast was the snatching of the *cocarde*—the red rag fixed to a string between the horns of each bull—Alex learned. But this was no mean achievement. Physical agility to the nth degree was called for, and if it fell short the young men going in the ring were the ones who would get hurt, not the bulls.

They sat on until a second run of bulls and horses raised the dust in the street, then made their way to the bull ring. There, in spite of her general feeling of frustration, Alex found herself beginning to be carried along on the excitement of the watching crowds as the *razeteurs* entered the ring, and one by one made the most daring and spectacular attempts to retrieve the coveted *cocarde*. There was a double barrier round the ring, and once or twice a bull got so carried away by its charge that it leapt the inner barrier after the *razeteur* and circled the narrow passageway before being let back into the contest area.

After the professionals, amateurs were invited in to try their skill, and the youths who had managed to unseat Alex were first into the ring.

'*Vous aussi, Anglais*?' they taunted Marcus, whose fair head made him an obvious target in the tiered seats.

'*C'est une invitation*?' he called back, getting to his feet, to the delight of the crowd.

'You're surely not rising to that crazy suggestion?' Alex protested.

'It's a friendly invitation. Where's your national pride?' he told her dismissively, and in seconds he was in the ring, being handed the metal hook each of the *razeteurs* used in the attempt to snatch the *cocarde*.

It was soon obvious how much skill had been demonstrated by the experts. Alex found herself holding the edge of her seat as she watched. One by one the amateurs owned themselves defeated and leapt out of the ring, until only Marcus and one other man remained. It was Marcus who held the eyes of the watching crowd as he wove and side-stepped, judging each move to the split-second.

Suddenly a delighted roar went up from the crowd. He had got the *cocarde*! In an instant he had leapt up on to the inner barrier, and was brandishing his trophy, then he strode across the gap to the outer barrier and stepped down, dropping the red *cocarde* into Alex's hands.

'The spoils for the lady,' he said. His suntanned skin was glistening evidence of the effort he had expended, as was the damp hair he tossed back.

Alex had been applauding and cheering as loudly as the rest, and when the boys who had so angered her shouted, '*Vive les Anglais!*' across the ring she actually waved the *cocarde* and laughed in acknowledgement before turning to Marcus. As her eyes met his, she realised with a shock of disgust just how carried away she had been. She had wanted him to win... had felt pride in him. She dropped back into her seat then, knowing that for the moment she had forgotten both who she was, and who Marcus was. Her sister and her father, silent, accusing ghosts, seemed to glide between them.

'Well done,' she said with dull politeness.

'Luck,' Marcus said simply. 'I think we'd better call it a day and end on a high note.'

'Better that than being upstaged.' Yes, that was better. That was a way of talking to him that left her feeling comfortable.

'Quite. And there's also the little matter of the meal we're due to eat back at the Mas. I don't want to inconvenience the Malmonts any more than we have done already.'

He didn't refer to the following day at all as they rode back to where the box had been left, and from there drove back to the Mas. And later, when they were seated round the huge dining-table with the other guests eating Henriette's mouthwatering *cassoulet* and *tarte aux pommes*, the conversation remained general. Alex let the babble of sound wash over her once Marcus became involved in conversation with the person on his other side. Tomorrow loomed over her, one huge question mark. Her brave talk of coping this morning seemed empty now as she contemplated borrowing money to get herself home. From whom, though? Anyone rather than Marcus Wakeford. But she was not exactly spoiled for choice.

At the end of the meal, Marcus turned to her.

'Well, isn't it about time you came to meet your charges?'

The implication of what he had said washed over her for a moment. 'There isn't a lot of point, is there?' she said, then stopped. '*Your charges*' he had said. Her green eyes were luminescent with hope. But dared she believe what she thought she had heard?

'You said . . . you called them my charges. Does that mean——'

'It means the horses you'll be helping to look after between here and England. What else?'

Relief washed over her. She was going to earn her return journey. She was not going to have to beg.

'But I came off Zizi,' she said.

'Of course you did,' he replied impatiently. 'If you hadn't, rearing as she did, your weight could have brought her down.'

Alex sighed with a mixture of relief and exasperation. 'You could have told me that *that* was what you thought at the time.'

He seemed genuinely amazed. 'It never occurred to me that you didn't realise that was what I was thinking. Come on!' He took her arm and led her away from the table.

In the shadowy paddock the two Camargues were white and ghostly, but they came over to the fence as soon as they heard Marcus calling them, and seemed eager to respond.

'This is Lasco. He's named after the Lascaux caves where his ancestors decorate the walls.' Marcus fondled the big horse's ears, a smile of complete gentleness on his face, the sort of smile that was light-years distant from the taunting expression he had through the day directed at her, Alex thought. 'And this dainty madam is Mistral.'

It was love at first sight as Alex caressed the small horse's velvety nose. The white head nodded as though in greeting, and the intelligent eyes were gentle as they watched her every move. The long white mane and tail were still now, but Alex could imagine how they would fly out in motion. She had completely fallen for both Camargues, and they at least would ensure that there was something bearable about the next few days.

It was not of the horses, however, that she found herself thinking as she lay in bed that night. Her mind replayed over and over, relentlessly, like a film loop, the scene in the bull ring with Marcus, lean, athletic, and utterly riveting to watch. She heard his voice again... 'The spoils for the lady', he had said, like some medieval knight after a jousting tournament.

Some joke that was, she told herself. He was no knight, willing to suffer for undying, courtly love. He was the man who ran away. The man who found love disappeared when the ground in which it grew proved unsuitable.

The red *cocarde* was on the table by her bed, glowing in a patch of moonlight coming in through the open shutters. Impatient with her obsessive thoughts, Alex got out of bed and dropped the piece of red cloth into her rubbish bin. Enough of that nonsense.

A sleepless quarter of an hour later, though, she was sneaking shamefacedly out to retrieve it. It was only a souvenir, after all. A souvenir of an occasion, not of a man. There was surely no harm in keeping it on those terms.

CHAPTER THREE

ALEX sat in the dining-room, tantalised by the smell of freshly baked bread. She might look cool and fresh in her yellow trousers and white baggy shirt, but there was no denying that she felt rather apprehensive about the next few days. Being on the road alone with Marcus would be vastly different from being here where there were people to defuse any tension between them. The room was quickly filling up with holiday-makers who didn't look to have a care in the world. She envied them their carefree laughter.

The red *cocarde* was burning a hole in her conscience. She had held it over the waste-paper basket in her room yet again this morning, but once more had given in to the urge to keep it. She had told herself that it would act as a reminder that its winner was symbolised by red for danger. But, maddeningly, the image of how he had looked when he won it refused to leave her mind.

She was asked if she wasn't eating and said that she was waiting for someone. On the stroke of eight Marcus came into the room, one hundred per cent rugged male, ready for action in jeans and navy round-necked T-shirt, his fair hair sleek and sculptured from his shower. Without looking round he went into the kitchen, coming out with a bowl of coffee, and took an empty place near the kitchen door.

Mortified at having waited for someone who obviously wasn't giving her a thought, Alex hung on for a moment or two, then made for the kitchen to get her own coffee. He was unaware of her as she came past, but was looking directly at her as she came out.

'Haven't you got an alarm clock?' he asked, looking pointedly at the hands of the wall clock which now stood at five past eight.

Alex coloured. 'I've been here some time.'

'Then why didn't you get on with it? Breakfast is self-service here. The Malmonts have quite enough to do with the horses at this time of day.'

'I thought perhaps I should wait for you.'

'No need to stand on ceremony.' He got up and pulled out the chair opposite to his. 'Sit down. I'll go over today's route with you.'

'I already have a seat over there,' Alex said mulishly.

'Then change it.' The steely grey eyes threatened trouble if she disobeyed, and, fuming inwardly, she sat down.

He sat opposite her, sipping black coffee and staring at her while she busied herself with buttering an end piece of loaf and spreading it with cherry jam, trying at the same time not to feel so tense.

'I suppose it's inevitable,' he said at last.

She looked across at him, and was momentarily disconcerted by the clear grey eyes, dark-fringed, surveying her at close quarters. 'What's inevitable?'

'That there should be moods to match the hair.'

Alex put down her knife with a clatter, irritation bubbling up again. 'If you only knew how tedious it is to be labelled by the colour of your hair. I wish to goodness——' She stopped suddenly and a cold sweat broke out over her. She had been going to say, I wish to goodness I'd been born a brunette like Elaine. She had come within a hair's breadth of blowing her cover. 'I wish people wouldn't,' she finished lamely, then added, 'I'd swap it for any colour in creation!'

'Green, for instance?' he asked laconically. 'Don't be foolish. If you've been given hair the colour of beech leaves in autumn it's not only ungrateful to divine providence—it's the height of stupidity to pretend you'd have it otherwise.'

Alex was wrong-footed by the almost complimentary phrasing, and took refuge in facetiousness.

'"Beech leaves in autumn"'! I suppose you mean dry and crackly!'

He gave her an unsmiling look. 'I thought nineties woman was above fishing for compliments.'

'And *I* thought *I* was unhooking one and throwing it back,' she said.

The grey eyes held hers for a moment. 'Ever get called "smart alec"? Or should I say "smart Alex"?' he asked, and before she could answer he put a map on the table and opened it up sideways on so that both of them could read it. 'Enough of nonsense. It's time we got to work. This is the route I hope we'll cover today.'

He traced the roads through Arles and Avignon to where they joined the *autoroute*, then north a little way.

'Provided things go well, we'll come off the motorway here at Loriol.'

He had nice hands, she was noticing, slim and brown, with long, tapering fingers. She couldn't stand stubby fingers. And his nails were well-shaped. Well cared-for too. She became aware of what she was doing, and reminded herself sharply of who he was. He might have nice hands, but he had a rotten lukewarm heart. She tuned in on what he was saying, prodding her concentration into life.

'The Malmonts have given me addresses to head for. Fortunately their riding contacts spread over quite a bit of France, so if we keep to schedule we'll not have to hunt around for a field to put the horses in—or ourselves, for that matter. I shan't want you to do any of the driving, but you can keep an eye on the map and make sure we're not going astray when we're not on the *autoroute*.'

'Fine.'

'Are you packed?'

'Absolutely ready.'

'I'll bring your bags down, then.'

'No need for that. I don't have a porter everywhere I go.'

'As you wish. Bring them over to the stables. No need to look for the Malmonts. They'll be over there.'

The Range Rover was already loaded with bales of hay, bags of horse nuts, plastic water carriers and buckets. Alex fitted her luggage in with some difficulty, aware of grey eyes watching her, and knowing that Marcus, who no doubt saw quite clearly that a bit of assistance might have been appropriate, was deliberately refraining from offering it a second time.

'Want to try out Mistral before she goes aboard?' he asked.

'If you're in no hurry.'

'I wouldn't have made the suggestion if that were the case,' he said with heavy patience.

They took the tack out of the Range Rover and went round to the paddock where Mistral and Lasco allowed themselves to be saddled.

'A couple of tips——' Marcus said as Alex was about to mount.

Her colour rose. 'Oh, come on! I thought I'd proved myself yesterday.' She sprang lightly into the saddle.

He looked up at her, his expression inscrutable. 'Go on, then.'

Alex pressed her knees into the little horse's flanks. Instantly, Mistral took off at the speed of light, like no other horse Alex had ever ridden, swerving at the fence and careering back towards Marcus, who had stepped discreetly but unhurriedly back out of the path of the whirlwind. Alex pulled on the reins, and equally suddenly Mistral halted in such a way that it was a miracle that her rider didn't sail over her head.

'The two little tips were—go easy on the reins, and go gently with your knees,' Marcus said with infuriating matter-of-factness. 'It might be advisable in future to take the time to listen and think before you act.'

The little horse was tossing her head, her white mane dazzling in the morning sun, and Alex could have sworn that there was laughter in the dark eye that rolled up at her.

Marcus sprang into Lasco's saddle and walked him off, as smooth as silk. Alex's second start was considerably better than her first.

'The thing about Camargues is that they are very responsive,' he told her, rubbing it in. 'The lightest touch conveys what you want. No need to pull on them as you might on a hard-mouthed old hack.'

'I think I shall remember that,' Alex said tightly.

After a good gallop both horses went into the box without objection. Alex felt that she was beginning to understand Mistral. And myself…she thought with some shame, making a mental resolution not to be so quick to fly off the handle in future.

Farewells and thanks said to the Malmonts, they set off, heading for Arles.

'When were you expected back?' Marcus asked when they had been on the road for quite a while. 'It has just occurred to me that the few days delay could mean you're late back for work. Should you call the hospital?'

'No problem. As a matter of fact, at the moment there isn't a hospital.'

He looked enquiringly at her.

'The cottage hospital where I worked has just closed. The old story—lack of funds.' Her voice reflected her sadness about the closing of the dear little hospital both she and the patients had loved so much.

'So you're out of work as well as out of money?'

'I'm not out of money. I just haven't got the means of getting hold of it at the moment. But yes, I am out of work, unfortunately.'

She heard the disapproval in his voice as he went on, 'Incredible! You lose your job, and waltz off on holiday as though you hadn't a care in the world.'

'Not really,' Alex said coldly. 'A certain amount of thought went into the decision. But I had booked this holiday and I saw no real reason to cancel it, or to let down the friends I've been riding with. And while I have been away I've given a good deal of thought to my future. I'm still not sure what I intend to do. In my field there are openings in industry, athletics and private practice as well as in the health service. I don't intend to rush into anything, since a change has been forced on me.'

He was silent for a moment, digesting this. Then he said, 'So you can do it.'

Alex looked puzzled. 'Do what?'

'Think first, act later.' He glanced sidelong at her. 'And give a reasoned answer without losing your temper.'

She bit back a contentious reply with some difficulty and looked determinedly out of the window.

'Open it if you're too hot,' he said, his face deadpan, and Alex knew that, though she might have controlled her words, the rush of angry colour to her cheeks had betrayed her.

'Is that Arles we can see in the distance?' she asked with careful steadiness. 'If it is, concentration's going to be called for. The map looks complicated.'

'I hope you're capable of giving a more informative interpretation of the map than that,' he said coldly.

'The place name comes over the centre. I can't do anything about that. Apart from saying that you need to follow the 570, I'm at a loss.'

'Just as well one of us isn't, then,' he said laconically.

They drew nearer to the lovely red circular town of Arles and both fell silent as Marcus drove unerringly through the historic city. Glimpses of the amphitheatre and other historic monuments flashed past, and eventually they were through and on the road to Avignon.

'Sorry,' Alex said briefly. 'I wasn't much use there.'

'At least you had the sense to keep quiet and not throw hysterical wrong instructions at me,' he said calmly. 'In any case, Arles I know. But you can swot up Avignon before we get there, if you like.'

Alex bent over the map, concentrating, her shining bright hair falling forward to screen her face. 'I think it looks fairly simple,' she said cautiously. 'And in any case——' her voice brightened '—there'll be signs for the *autoroute*, won't there? All we'll need to do is follow them.'

A hand came out to scoop back her hair, and Marcus looked pityingly at her. 'Forget the map. I never yet met a woman who could read one. Let's just hope you can do better with the horses. You might as well put your head back and leave me to get on with it. We'll stop at the first service station on the *autoroute* to stretch our legs.'

Seething with unspoken retorts, Alex put her head back and closed her eyes but she didn't go to sleep. She was too busy brooding on how malign fate was to have brought her and Marcus together. Could it be for some purpose? The possibility of some kind of revenge on Elaine's behalf floated into her mind. She would never again have such an opportunity, but the trouble was that Marcus held all the cards. He was the boss. He had the money and the means of getting back to England, while she was dependent on him for everything. No doubt if she displeased him too much he wouldn't hesitate to dump her at the roadside. She wriggled, frustrated by the thought.

'Uncomfortable?'

She opened her eyes but was careful not to look at him. 'No, not at all. Just restless.' She watched the hot road unrolling in front of them, promising herself that if a good opportunity presented itself she would seize it. She owed it to her sister.

They had to park in the heavy vehicles section at the service area, and took it in turns to go off and find refreshments so that the horses were not left unguarded.

Marcus went first, at Alex's insistence, and she opened the door wide and sat on the Range Rover's step, her eyes closed and her face turned up to the sun.

'Take your horses on holiday with you, do you?'

She opened her eyes to see a young British lorry driver opening up the cab of the vehicle next to them.

'Not so much take them as bring them back,' she said. 'They're presents from the seaside.'

'Some presents!'

'Some seaside!'

He grinned at her. 'All right for some. All I get to do is shift breakfast cereals.'

'Better than moving them around England in the rain, though.' A wide sweep of her arm indicated the blue skies and sunshine.

'True.' He leaned against his cab, prepared to talk. 'What's your name? Mine's Gary.'

He was friendly as a puppy, with an open face, not the unpleasantly pushy type at all. 'Alex,' she said.

'Alex . . .' he repeated, considering. 'That's nice. Want a piece of chocolate?' He reached into the cab and brought out a familiar British bar, breaking off a piece.

'I don't believe this!' Alex eyed the make. 'Which came first, the brand preference, or the television advert?'

She was taking the offered piece and they were both laughing when Marcus appeared round the front of the Range Rover, his face full of disapproval.

'I'm back,' he said curtly. 'You can go now.'

'I will, in a minute, when I've eaten my chocolate,' she said carelessly. 'You've heard of lorry drivers and Yorkie bars? Here's the original.'

'Really? You won't be too long, will you?' he said pointedly.

Alex stiffened. The lorry driver's eyes went from one to the other of them, his face amused at Marcus's disapproval.

'I'll be as quick as is humanly possible,' she told Marcus, turning slightly so that he was excluded, since his only interest seemed to be in terminating the harmless exchange of pleasantries. 'How long does the trip up to the coast take you, Gary?'

'All being well, I shall make the last crossing from Calais tonight. Which reminds me, I'd better be on my way if I don't want to miss it.' Tactfully he turned aside with a cheery wave.

Alex waited to wave him off, just to make her point, then without another look at Marcus headed for the service buildings. He had been insufferably rude just now, and it would serve him right if she kept him waiting. Wisely, though, once she had had a few minutes to calm down in the coffee queue, she decided that it would not be diplomatic to hang around too long. In no more than fifteen minutes, she was back at the car.

Marcus was reading a French newspaper he must have bought in the shop. As she got in, he passed it over to her, indicating an article with a lurid headline about a murderer who had struck once on the *autoroute* and was thought likely to repeat the offence.

'Tell me if you need it translated,' he said briefly.

'My French is adequate enough for me to see what it's about. I've no desire to read it in detail,' she told him.

'You should. It might convince you that it isn't exactly advisable to let any Tom, Dick or Harry pick you up when you're on the road.'

'It wasn't a question of picking up. Gary was a perfectly harmless, friendly British lorry driver, just wanting to say hello to a fellow countryman.'

'*Woman,*' he corrected significantly. 'And even the foulest murderer has been known to speak pleasantly to the next-door neighbour, remember.'

She laughed disbelievingly. 'He was only offering me a piece of chocolate, for goodness' sake!'

'Did no one ever warn you never to accept sweets from strangers?'

'Yes—when I was a child. It may have escaped your notice, but I am no longer in the pre-school age-group.'

His eyes swept over her. 'It hadn't escaped my notice,' he said shortly, but the way he said it summoned the angry colour to her cheeks again.

'If you go on about it much longer,' she said, 'I shall begin to think I have as much cause to be worried about you as you think you have to be worried about a perfectly innocent stranger.'

'A bit of prudent wariness wouldn't come amiss.' He shifted so that he could sit round sideways and give her the full benefit of his piercing grey stare. 'I've told you already that I think you assume far too easily that a course of action is safe. This might suit you very well, but at the moment you're in my charge. I would be grateful if you wouldn't attach yourself to every stray male who comes within sniffing distance.'

'Do you realise how incredibly rude that sounds?' Alex asked hotly.

'Of course. I meant it to have a certain impact.'

She looked away from him, staring straight ahead through the windscreen. 'Well, your efforts are all quite unnecessary. I know how to take care of myself. I've made sure of that.'

'And what does that mean?'

'It means that I've been through a series of self-defence classes.' She gave him a brief, significant glance. 'Anyone having ideas of making me the subject of an article like this lurid one you've shown me would have quite a surprise, I can assure you.'

'Sounds good. But I would prefer not to see proof of it.' He switched on the engine, indicating that as far as he was concerned the matter was settled and the subject closed. Very smoothly, his mind as aware of the horses' comfort as it had appeared to be concerned about her safety, they drew away from the parking space and headed for the *autoroute* again.

That had all sounded very responsible, very rough-diamond chivalrous—if chivalry could be cloaked in such rudeness, Alex thought. What it was far more likely to indicate, though, was that the illustrious Mr Wakeford was not used to any female turning her head away from him and towards someone else in trousers. Well, they would see about that. She had no intention of obeying that kind of order. She might be working for him, but she was not having her whole personality moulded by him. Especially not by him.

Private thoughts occupied both of them for several miles until Alex felt that someone had to break the silence, and it might as well be her.

'Won't Mistral and Lasco find life a bit limited as pet ponies?' she asked. 'I mean—Camargues are used to working, aren't they?'

'They'll work for me. I keep sheep.'

'You're a farmer?'

'You sound surprised.'

She was. Elaine had told her he was an accountant, but that was an explanation she couldn't give.

'I had you down for one of the professions,' she said non-committally.

'Well, I'm only a part-time farmer. It's more of a hobby, but a demanding one. Rounding up the sheep and checking up on them when they're spread out over the South Downs should be enough to give Mistral and Lasco a sense of purpose.'

'So if that's your hobby, what's your real job?'

'Adding up. Or rather, making sure that other people add up properly. I have my own firm of accountants with branches spread over the south-east.'

'That's more the sort of thing I pictured you doing.'

'Dry and dusty?'

'Now who's being a smart alec?' she asked sweetly.

He slanted a cool grey look at her. 'Nothing smart about that. I merely understand how your mind works.'

That was a state of affairs that gave no comfort. Alex returned to the safer subject of the map. 'Only one more exit to go, then we shall be at Loriol,' she told him.

'In that case, I suggest we settle for a late lunch when we arrive at this place the Malmonts have picked out rather than stopping on the roadside.'

'That's fine by me.'

'As soon as we leave the *autoroute*, keep your eyes skinned for a shop where we can pick up something for a picnic lunch tomorrow morning. It will help if we don't have to do too much hunting around before getting on the road again. We're provided for today. Henriette gave me a hamper that looks as though it could feed a dozen people.'

'You don't know the extent of my appetite!'

'If it were more than a normal healthy one, those jodhpurs of yours wouldn't have managed to keep the results of any excesses secret.'

Alex blinked, but held her tongue. She had not been aware that he was inspecting anything but her riding ability yesterday.

They noted several useful-looking shops in the villages they went through, and soon came to the riding stables where they were to spend the night.

They were given a friendly welcome and directed to a paddock where Mistral and Lasco could be safely al-

lowed to run free. The owner apologised for the fact
that there were no available bedrooms, but offered them
the use of any of the bathrooms in the house as long as
they chose the hour between seven and eight when guests
would be in the dining-room. He told them of several
restaurants in the area, and listed places of interest they
might like to go and have a look at, then hurried off,
leaving them to see to the horses and set up camp.

It was much easier to relax when there was something
to do, Alex thought as they set about the various tasks.
They both watched with pleasure as the horses, delighted to be out of the box again, kicked up their heels
and raced around the field, full of the joy of freedom.
By the time the picnic lunch was spread out, Alex was
feeling more at ease than she had been at any point up
to now, and actually found herself talking to Marcus
without weighing every word she uttered.

Henriette had certainly gone to town on the picnic
lunch. There was a delicious onion tart, with huge juicy
tomatoes to go with it, more of the morning's bread, a
variety of cheeses, and a basket of fruit. Marcus brought
out a bottle of Clairette de Die from a cool-bag, and the
dappled sunlight through the leaves of the tree they sat
under at the edge of the paddock was the final touch to
lull Alex into being more herself—dangerously herself—
and totally unaware of it.

So when Marcus suddenly said, 'You know, you
remind me of someone, but I'm damned if I know who,'
it came as a terrible shock. Alex knew that while she
might not look very much like her sister there were the
inevitable similarities of expression, the mannerisms
common to the family. Such things could betray almost
as easily as physical likeness.

'I must have a pretty universal kind of face,' she said,
recovering as quickly as she could. 'I'm always being
told that I have a double somewhere.'

He was staring at her, frowning, his grey eyes thoughtful. 'No, it's not the way you look. It's more the—the sort of atmosphere of you, if that doesn't sound corny. I just feel that we've met before... We haven't, I know. I'm sure I wouldn't have forgotten that hair if we had.'

'No. We've never met.' She was glad that she could say that with utter conviction. But how to put him off further? 'I'm Sussex born and bred. Are you? Perhaps it's just a similarity of background.'

'Maybe so.' He looked unconvinced but he let the dangerous subject drop, to her relief. 'More fruit?'

'I couldn't eat another thing.' She jumped to her feet, glad of the chance to get moving again. 'I'll clear these things away.'

'There's a bowl and water in the back of the Range Rover. While you do that, I'll see to our sleeping quarters.'

She had not really given much thought to that, but now, as she got on with the small amount of washing-up, Alex knew that no way would she share a tent with this man. If that was his idea, then he could think again. She would empty every bale of straw and bag of horse nuts out of the car and sleep in there—or under the tree. She was prepared not to make difficulties to some extent, but sharing a tent with him was beyond her limit.

What she saw when he called her over to the Range Rover, though, was not a tent, but two hammocks slung from a tree to opposited ends of the car.

'There we are. Who needs bedrooms?' he said, giving one of the hammocks a push so that it swung violently.

'Firstly, what happens if it rains? And secondly, I've never slept in a hammock,' she said warily.

'Well, tonight's your chance to find out what it's like. As for the prospect of rain, you can forget that. The paper I prudently bought assures me that we're going to have to go on putting up with sun and cloudless skies at least until we cross the Channel.'

'I'm relieved to hear that. But a "thirdly" has occurred to me. What happens if you turn over in your sleep?'

'You either do it right, or you fall out.' He gave a slight smile, and she thought with a shock, That's the first time he's done that directly at me. 'Surprisingly, it doesn't happen often,' he went on. 'You never fall out of bed, do you?'

'No. But the bed's got four feet on the ground. Oh, well, we shall see!' She was mentally resolving that if his head was towards the tree hers would be towards the Range Rover. She didn't want to be eyeball to eyeball with him in the moonlight. The picture that conjured up was so grotesque as to be funny. She gave a little involuntary private chuckle at the thought, and at once he said with a frown,

'There it is again, the feeling that I know you.'

'You do—for at least twenty-four hours now,' she said tetchily.

'No need to get grumpy again. You were beginning to be almost human.'

'Didn't anyone ever tell you that it's not exactly pleasing for a girl to be told that she's more or less one of a production run—not an individual with a claim to being unique?'

'No. But in any case, twenty-four hours with you had convinced me that there isn't much apart from a four-legged animal of the equine species that does please you. So I suggest we take the horses out for the afternoon; it's likely to lead to less controversy than conversation.'

'Nothing I'd like more,' Alex said crisply.

They were back to square one again, and square one was the safe place to be, she thought as they saddled Mistral and Lasco. Not for a Wakeford and a Leeward the pleasant chat and cosy friendship other men and women could enjoy. They were chalk and cheese, cat and dog, North and South Pole. She would do well never to forget it.

When they came back after a couple of hours' riding, the next hour was spent carefully picking out the horses' feet and feeding and watering them. Then Marcus settled himself in one of the hammocks with a brief announcement that he was going to indulge in a siesta. Alex got a paperback out of her bag and went to sit under one of the trees. She was not going to experiment with the hammock for the first time with those cool grey eyes looking on in amusement.

It was very hot, and inevitably there were inquisitive flies. Alex waved them away as she read, longing for the sea they had left behind.

She raised her head, becoming aware of a sound that she had not noticed until now when all was still. Running water. There must be a stream near by—or maybe even a river. There was nothing she would like more than a swim to cool down. A paddle would be better than nothing.

She glanced across at the hammock. Marcus was very still, his *gardian's* hat tilted over his eyes and partially covering his face. She watched the gentle rise and fall of his chest, sure that he was fast asleep.

She went cautiously over to the Range Rover, careful not to move anything in such a way that it would set the vehicle rocking, and managed to extricate her bathing costume from her bag. Then, with another quick glance at the sleeping figure, she made for the gate in the paddock and climbed over it so that there should be no creak to rouse Marcus. She needed a little time alone.

The path led away to the left through an orchard, then into another small field at the far side of which she could see the flash of water. The river at the point where she arrived at it was shallow and noisy, which accounted for the fact that she had heard it over quite a distance. But when she walked along the path she soon reached a place where the banks were higher, the river narrower, and the water deep enough to swim in, though not so deep that she couldn't see the stony bed and know that it was safe enough. There was no house and no human being in sight. Quickly Alex changed into her bathing costume and did a shallow dive into the water.

It was delicious. She swam upstream against the gentle movement of the water, then back again to venture further downstream. A little flotilla of ducks approached her, inspected her with beady eyes, and passed on. When she floated on her back for a little while, letting the river take her along with it, her stillness was rewarded with the brilliant flash of blue as a kingfisher darted down to the water a little further upstream. Alex felt refreshed in both body and spirit when she eventually decided that welcome coolness was becoming coldness, and reluctantly got out at the point where she had left her clothes.

She had forgotten to bring a towel, but by the time she had walked under this powerful afternoon sun as far as the orchard she would be dry and able to change back into her clothes. She slipped her sandals on, and, picking up her things, headed back towards the paddock.

She only just managed to get her trousers and shirt on before she saw Marcus open the paddock gate and come out into the orchard to stare around. It took no second glance to detect that he was in the grip of formidable displeasure.

'Where have you been?' he demanded.

'Swimming. There's a lovely river down there.'

'Is it too much to ask that you should make your intentions known?' His voice was far more chilling than the water of the river. She must remember to annoy him again when she felt in need of being cooled down, Alex thought flippantly.

'You were asleep. I didn't think it necessary to wake you—nor did I think you would appreciate it.'

'Don't you mean that you never gave it a second's thought? You just took off the moment the idea occurred to you.'

Alex had had enough. It was high time they got this issue of what she could and couldn't do cleared up. 'Is there any reason why I shouldn't? It seemed like free time, and as far as I was concerned I thought I was justified in using it as such. I wasn't aware that I was supposed to watch you sleep, I'm afraid. That particular duty didn't feature in your little introductory talk.'

His jaw tightened. 'Do me a favour and cut out the flippancy. I thought I'd got this point across to you earlier on today, but apparently not. As long as you are in my employment, I am responsible for you. I want to know where you are, and what you are doing. Is that clear?'

'It's clear, but it's also highly unnecessary.' Alex began to walk away. 'I grew out of the need for a nanny years ago.'

He seized her arm, stopping her. 'And you haven't got one now,' he said. 'You've got a man, taking a man's responsibilities seriously.'

For a moment green eyes and angry grey ones locked, then Alex shook herself free from his hand.

'All right. Point taken, if not fully understood. In future, I'll rouse you from the deepest sleep to make my intentions known.'

'Oh, no, you won't,' he said with quelling firmness. 'You'll wait until I'm awake before you take it into your head to do anything.'

'Very well,' she said stiffly. 'Is there anything else?'

'Yes. If you want to take advantage of the offer of a bath, now's the time to do it. I shall do likewise, and then we'll go and find somewhere to eat.'

'How nice,' Alex said with false enthusiasm. And I just hope there isn't any cream in the vicinity or it'll be bound to turn sour, she added mentally.

Marcus was back at the paddock before her, and she saw that while she had put back on the yellow trousers and white shirt she had been wearing all day he had changed into well-fitting grey trousers and a matching fine cotton shirt, the cool colour a perfect foil for his tanned skin and fair hair—something which no doubt had not escaped his notice.

'You've changed,' she said, stating the obvious. 'I hadn't realised that we were going anywhere special.'

He raised his eyebrows. 'I hardly think any friend of the Malmonts would direct us to a transport café. And before you start firing on all cylinders, that remark was not intended to imply any criticism of what you're wearing. You'll do as you are.'

Alex had no intention of meriting such lukewarm comments on her appearance. 'I'd rather be a little more suitable,' she told him firmly. 'You'll have to go and watch the horses for a moment to give me time to change, though.'

'Trust a woman to make a fuss over clothes,' he said, rather unfairly in the circumstances, but he strolled away to stand at some distance, his back towards her.

Alex ferreted in her bag, knowing exactly what she was looking for. She had made two pre-holiday purchases that had cost her an arm and a leg and a little bit more, but both had repaid well by allowing her to roll them up, put them in a plastic bag and stuff them anyhow into her case, and take them out days later to find them without a single crease.

She took out the jade-green halter-neck dress now, and quickly changed into it. Then, slipping into the Range Rover's passenger seat and flicking down the mirror, she quickly pinned back her hair with two antique combs someone had given her for her last birthday. A touch of the pale lipstick that best suited her colouring, and she was ready. She called over to Marcus and told him as much.

He came back, and gave her a slow head-to-toe look.

'Expecting the Ritz?' he said briefly. A compliment or an insult? Alex couldn't care less. Even if it was his idea of a compliment, he could toss it to the four winds and she wouldn't lift a finger to catch it.

The little restaurant which they reached after driving up through the rounded green foothills of the Vercors was perched on the side of a precipitous slope. There were panoramic views out over the rolling countryside below from their table on a terrace whose walls were heavy with bougainvillaea. As they ate darkness fell, but the scene over which they looked was no less lovely as lights starred the floor of the valley, mirroring those in the sky above, and the last traces of the spectacular sunset lingered, silhouetting the jagged mountain peaks.

The waiter who served them seemed to jump to the conclusion that they were a genuine couple, and nothing Marcus did served to disillusion him. Indeed, Marcus behaved with such apparent charm and easy good humour that even Alex fell prey to it and managed to forget for a while that this evening was something she should be enduring, not enjoying.

As they savoured each successive dish from the wonderful menu, and drank the wines Marcus chose, Alex grew more and more animated, more like the Alex her friends knew and not the prickly, defensive creature that being with Marcus Wakeford had turned her into.

Marcus reacted to her glowing face and bright, laughing eyes in such a way that it was not surprising that their relationship was wrongly assessed, not only by the waiter but by others whose eyes were drawn to Alex's vivid head. Both of them enjoyed the evening far more than they had anticipated.

As they went out of the restaurant, other customers were coming in, and Marcus put his arm round Alex to draw her aside against the terrace wall so that people could pass. Instead of letting her go, his grip tightened as he turned her round to look out over the valley so that he could point to a shooting star that dazzled across the sky.

'Wish! You'll never have a better chance!' he said.

They were alone now for a moment, and they watched the star die away in silence.

'Did you?' he asked softly.

Alex had not so much formulated a wish as felt a vague yearning—a regret that the atmosphere of the meal they had just shared had been false, that he was who he was, and she was someone who should never have been able to pretend that she was enjoying being with him, not even for the sake of appearances. Because she had been pretending, hadn't she?

She looked up at him, reluctant to answer. 'Not really,' she said slowly.

'That makes two of us. Difficult to think of anything to wish for at the moment, isn't it? It's been a good evening,' he said. 'Thank you for sharing it with me.'

Then, while she still looked up at him, locked into her bittersweet thoughts, he drew her closer and kissed her... and she let him. It felt as though he was trying to kiss the shadows from her eyes, the threat of sadness from the curve of her lips.

She realised with a wave of guilt that she was not making any attempt to withdraw, and she stiffened in his arms, rigid with shame and disloyalty. What was she doing? What was she thinking of? How could she?

'Cold?' he asked.

'A bit. Tired, too.' Space and mountain air between them restored her to sanity but didn't remove the pall of guilt.

Afterwards when she sat silently beside him as they drove through the darkness back to the riding stables she thought that those few seconds had been the most foolish of her life. While his lips were warm on her eyelids and mouth, she had felt, This is real. Not the distant family past with its bitterness and rancour. Not, though she was ashamed to think it, the more recent hurt and rejection suffered by Elaine. Not even the damage to her father's health—and that was the most shaming thought of all. Nothing had seemed more real than that moment—and she had wanted it to go on forever.

It hadn't, of course. It had died as the shooting star had died, and now she was regretting it, fully aware of her mental betrayal of her sister and her father. Marcus was regretting it too, she felt. He was as withdrawn now as she was, and whatever had flared between them existed no longer. She was glad, she told herself fiercely. After all, what had it been but a bit of ephemeral night magic?

Back in the dark paddock, with the ghostly figures of Mistral and Lasco swaying drowsily near the hedge, she was relieved when Marcus said that he was going over to the house to see about his bill so that they could get an early start in the morning.

She was quixotically glad, too, when her hammock threw her out on to the hard ground at her first attempt to get into it. This is where I should be, she told herself, glad to be some kind of martyr, even a comic one. Back down to earth, feet and all the rest of me well and truly on the ground. She was more successful at her second attempt, and by the time Marcus came back she was tucked into her sleeping-bag, not asleep, but able to answer his, 'Are you comfortable?' with a drowsy murmur that said as plainly as words that she had no intention of being disturbed.

She heard him moving around, preparing for bed, and then grunting with the effort of getting his long legs into his own sleeping-bag. After a moment or two, he said softly, 'Goodnight, Alex.'

She murmured an incoherent goodnight, and then there was silence apart from the occasional blowing breath of Mistral and Lasco, and the rustlings of the night world.

Alex felt safe again, cocooned in her sleeping-bag, her eyes and her mind closed to the mysterious, treacherous witchcraft of stars and sunsets. Tomorrow there would be the bright light of day when you saw quite clearly exactly where you were going. Her lips tightened with resolve as she thought, *And with whom.*

CHAPTER FOUR

ALEX opened her eyes to find Mistral's head nuzzling her, blowing warm breath on her neck. She wriggled an arm free of her sleeping-bag, and rubbed the white nose before gently pushing the little horse away.

She realised that there was movement beyond the other hammock and adjusted her position cautiously so that she could see what was going on.

Marcus was getting dressed. She lay prudently still, watching the smooth bronze curve of his back as he stooped to pull on his jeans. His legs, as brown as his back, were well-muscled, his thighs long and powerful. He had slept in the briefest of underwear, something she had contemplated doing herself. Now, conscious of the sneaky once-over she was giving him, and realising that had she been first out of bed the same treatment would no doubt have been meted out to her, she was glad of the cotton pyjamas she had on. But she went on looking.

If you were assessing him on purely physical grounds, he was certainly a most attractive man. As he fastened the belt of his jeans, she was fascinated by the movement of the muscles of his back under that bronzed, velvety skin. And there was the way the early morning sun struck gold from the hair on his arms as he moved.

She became fully aware of the nature of what she was feeling as she looked at him, and burrowed down into her sleeping-bag, blotting out the sight of him.

Oh, Elaine . . . she thought desperately. What a rotten sister I am. I know all he has done to you, and I find myself as near as dammit to fancying the man. What's wrong with me? First last night, and now before I'm

71

fully awake here I am ogling the man like any common voyeur. I'm despicable.

'Awake, are you?' He was standing close to her hammock, and she had the option of meeting eyes she would prefer not to meet right now, or looking at his upper half—still stripped to the waist.

She took refuge in rubbing her eyes so that she didn't have to look at any part of him. 'Only just.'

'How did you sleep?'

She yawned.

'Not long enough, apparently,' he said ironically. The light behind him was having the effect of creating a nimbus round that dazzling fair head of his. He looked like some kind of sun god—sun devil, she corrected herself, closing her eyes against the sight of him.

'What time is it?' she muttered with affected sleepiness.

'Six o'clock—but don't blame me for waking you. Blame Mistral. However, since we are awake, there's no point in hanging around. If, that is,' he added with heavy irony, 'you ever manage to get your eyes open.'

He had moved away and was reaching for his sponge bag which he had hung on a branch of the tree the hammock was attached to. Alex wriggled herself upright and contemplated the next move.

'How on earth do you get out of this thing?' she asked, panicking as the hammock rocked wildly.

He gave her a mocking look. 'With prudence. Impulsive movements are definitely not on.'

Alex waited until he was almost at the gate, then attempted to extract herself from both sleeping-bag and hammock at the same time. The hammock cheated and flung her on to the ground on all fours, her sleeping-bag on top of her. She tossed it aside, and glanced apprehensively across the field to see Marcus watching her from the other side of the gate.

'Go on, laugh!' she called crossly, all feeling of physical attraction towards him dissipated. 'It would have been more civilised of you to give a sensible answer to a question in the first place. The wretched thing did that when I attempted to get in last night as well.'

'Remind me to give you a demonstration tonight,' Marcus said, his face deadpan. 'I didn't realise it was such a problem.'

She was so angry for a number of reasons that she scrambled to her feet forgetting all about the hammock and found her face netted in its web. She heard a disbelieving, 'What next?' from over by the gate, but by the time she had extricated herself Marcus had gone.

At least it was safer to be a buffoon than an object of romantic interest, she thought savagely, rolling up the sleeping-bags and stowing them in the Range Rover.

She armed herself with her own toilet things and clean clothes, and walked over to the gate to watch impatiently for Marcus's return.

When she came back from the house, fresh and neat in jeans and a navy and cream striped Breton shirt, her mood as cool as her appearance, Marcus had saddled both horses.

'We may as well give them a bit of a work-out before we leave,' he said amiably. 'They'll go into the box all the more willingly, and with luck we'll come across somewhere with fresh croissants and coffee on offer.'

'As you like. Have you locked the car?'

'No.' He tossed her the keys. 'Do it, will you, if you're putting your things in? Thanks for stowing the bedding, by the way.'

'It's what I'm here for, isn't it?' she said, her voice clipped.

He was looking assessingly at her as she came back to Mistral and handed him the keys.

'Reverted to feeling like that today, have you?'

'I don't know what you mean.'

'Oh, yes, you do. Last night you were almost human.'

She gave him a cold look. 'Last night I had rather a lot to drink.'

'Without which, wild horses wouldn't have dragged a smile out of you, never mind the odd kiss. That's to-day's explanation, is it?'

'Since you mention it,' she said, looking directly at him, 'I would prefer no repetition of that particular part of last night to occur.'

'No more wine?' She could tell by the light in his eyes that he was deliberately misunderstanding her.

'No more "odd kisses",' she said crisply. If he wanted it absolutely straight, then he could have it. 'You cast doubt on my wisdom in embarking on this trip with someone I don't know. Well, I'm wise enough to know that you could misinterpret what happened last night. I was completely taken by surprise. Please let's have no further embarrassment for either of us.'

'Well, blow me down...' he said sarcastically. 'And there was I deluding myself you'd actually kissed me back. What strange forms surprised passivity can take.'

Alex's face went a rapid scarlet, then pale. 'Be as facetious as you like, but I'm telling you quite clearly that I want no repetitions. From now on, we concentrate on the horses. You're employing me to look after them— nothing more.'

His expression was almost pitying as he said, 'If I'd had the least idea that you would so misinterpret a casual kiss in appreciation of a combination of things—good food, wonderful scenery, company that had turned out less of a drag than expected—I would have refrained from causing you such maidenly distress.' He folded his arms and stood looking scornfully at her. 'You attach a surprising amount of importance to something that meant very little. Believe me, I'd have kissed my grand-mother, if I'd had one and she'd been there.'

'I've made my point.' But he was cutting her down to size by stressing how unimportant a point it was. Alex could feel her colour rising again. 'If it seems silly to you,' she went on with as much self-possession as she could muster, 'Then I can assure you it's no more ridiculous than the embargo you've put on my moving two steps away from you. We shall just have to learn to tolerate each other's idiosyncrasies.'

She gave a hot-headed leap into Mistral's saddle, forgot all yesterday's riding instructions, and caused the little horse to shoot off like a bat out of hell once again. When she had completed a wild circuit of the paddock and returned to the starting point, Marcus said crisply, 'It's to be hoped I learn tolerance more quickly than you learn to ride a Camargue.'

There was no reply to outsmart that, so Alex made for the gate, her touch on Mistral gentle, her thoughts about Marcus the exact opposite. However, the point about any romantic opportunities their situation might offer had been made, and, pour scorn on the idea as he might, she thought it more likely than not that he would take it on board. No more false emotions engendered by stars and moonlight. No more forgetting who her employer was, no matter how much he might switch on the charm.

He passed her and spurred Lasco on to a gallop. Alex followed suit, glad of the wind in her hair to blow any trace of last night's cobwebs away.

They found a bar open in one of the villages they passed through, and tethered the horses to a solid-looking seat in the little square.

'And in case you have any misgivings, I never go in for seduction over breakfast,' Marcus said while they waited for their bowls of coffee and croissants at an outside table.

'Let it drop, Marcus,' she replied. 'I think we both know the score.'

The sun was warm now as the shops and houses came to life. Mistral gave a sudden, rasping cough, and they both looked over at her.

'Has she been doing that while we were riding?' Marcus asked, frowning.

Alex considered. 'Only when we first set off, I think. I blamed myself for that—giving her such a stupid kick-start.'

'Keep an alert ear to check if it goes on, will you? I don't want her developing anything.'

They carried on eating, their attention half on the horses, but no further coughing occurred.

'Oh, look,' Alex said, 'the grocer's shop is open now, over there, next to the *boulangerie*. If you like, I could go over and get something for lunch.'

'It would save a stop. I'll see to the bill here while you do that.'

She stood waiting, embarrassed, until he looked up at her.

'What's the matter? Do you want more coffee?' he asked. 'I thought you'd finished.'

'No, I don't want more coffee. I—I need some money. I haven't got any, remember.'

'Of course you haven't. Here——' He brought folded notes from the back pocket of his jeans and gave them to her, then, seeing how awkward the little transaction made her feel, he said impatiently, 'No need to look like that. I forgot, that's all. Get on with it.'

Still feeling as though she had been caught begging, Alex set off across the square, conscious again of how dependent she was on Marcus Wakeford. She couldn't even buy herself an aspirin if she got a headache. What a ridiculous, maddening situation.

She bought bread and slices of Paris ham, half a box of Camembert, and a pound of apricots, then went over to Marcus who had returned to the horses. She told him what she had got. 'I wondered about butter, but thought it would melt. And I didn't get anything to drink.'

'That's fine. I've got both butter and wine in a cool-box in the car.'

'Here's your change. You gave me far too much. The bread was sixty francs, and——'

'I don't want an itemised bill. Put the change in this, and keep it in your pocket, if there's room for it.' He held something out towards her, his eyes appraising the snug fit of her jeans.

Apprehensively she took a little package from him, neatly wrapped in fine black paper and tied with gold string. 'What's this?'

'Open it and find out.'

She pulled on the string, and opened up the paper to find a little purse in soft black leather, with two compartments closing with delicate gold clasps. She examined it, her face unrevealing, then looked up at him. 'There was no need for this. I have pockets. I didn't need a purse.'

'Put the rest of the money you had to ask for so painfully just now in it, then I shall be spared your blushes tomorrow.' When she still hesitated, looking down at his gift, he said briskly, 'It takes more than a tuppenny-halfpenny purse to buy a woman, if that's what's running through your tiny mind. What you are holding is a manifestation of pure selfishness on my part. Now you can be entirely responsible for lunchtime provisions as we travel, and I shan't need to give them a thought. Nor shall I have to watch another of those ridiculous displays of embarrassment. Well—are you going to stand there forever?'

Alex stowed the remaining notes and coins in the purse and then met his eyes as she slipped it into her pocket and blushed again.

'Oh, throw the damned purse away if it makes you feel better,' he said with heavy false patience. 'I really don't care one way or the other.'

As she followed him on Mistral, Alex's eyes rested thoughtfully on his back. Taken at face value, that had been a quite unnecessary but rather nice thing to do, and it had left her feeling unsettled. It would be so much easier to remember who he was, and what he had done, if he behaved consistently badly. She frowned. But then, Elaine had spoken of him as being a thoroughly attractive person in every way—until he had found out who she was. She slipped her fingers into her pocket to feel the little purse, and frowned again. What on earth would he say if she told him that he had given a present to a Leeward? No doubt the charm would slip a bit. She straightened up and gently urged Mistral forward to make up ground she had lost while she daydreamed. Thank goodness he didn't know, and she was definitely not going to tell him.

Back at the field, Mistral coughed once or twice again while she was working her way through the ration of horse nuts she had been given.

Alex's eyes met Marcus's. 'Perhaps she's just choking on some food,' she said without conviction.

'And perhaps pigs might fly,' he said curtly. 'Do me a favour. Don't make consoling remarks. If the horse is going to be sick, she's going to be sick, and no amount of looking on the bright side will change it.'

Alex picked up the water carriers. If she couldn't manage to say the right thing, then she'd do something useful. But that move, too, met with disapproval.

He took one of the containers from her. 'No need to be a martyr. That won't improve matters either.' His tone was ungracious.

'Nor will jumping down my throat,' she said with some justification, she felt. She stomped off towards the tap in the yard, followed by Marcus in grim silence.

They had joined the *autoroute* and travelled fifty miles or so, still in the same silence, before he spoke another word.

'I suppose you think an apology's necessary. Is that what's needed for you to open your mouth again?'

'No,' she said levelly. 'I'm just letting you fester in peace.'

He shifted tetchily in the driving seat. 'All right. I concede that I was less than civil back there. I just want everything to be as I'd planned when I get back home with the horses. Leading in a coughing wreck wasn't on the cards.'

The pampered brat, of course. And the 'suitable' wife. Alex wasn't going to waste any sympathy on them.

'Surely no one is going to blame you for an illness?' she said, her tone of voice conveying her feelings with undisguised accuracy.

'It isn't a matter of blame. This was to be a very special occasion. A dream come true. I want it to be a perfect dream, not a semi-nightmare.'

'I'm out of my league,' she said drily. 'I've never had dreams come true on that kind of scale.'

'And you don't see why anyone else should either, is that it?'

He redirected his scowl from the road ahead to her and she decided that unless they were going to spend the journey in conflict she had better do something to encourage a more positive attitude.

'Look—it's probably nothing to worry about,' she told him firmly. 'And if it is, wouldn't it be more useful to see a vet rather than brood and row about it?'

He sighed resignedly after a moment and seemed to relax. 'The voice of wisdom. You're right, of course.' This time when he looked at her he seemed prepared to switch moods. 'Do something to take my mind off it, then. Tell me about your family, your boyfriend, anything. Just talk. I've had enough of silence.'

Red lights flashed in Alex's brain. Family. There was not much *détente* to be found in that direction. 'It's a very ordinary family,' she said dismissively. 'Mother and father enjoying early retirement, sister married with a baby, all of us happy and contented. No headline stuff, I'm glad to say.' Had her voice wobbled at the mention of Elaine? Or at the mention of her father's retirement? She thought not. And he had obligingly moved on to the next topic.

'And the boyfriend situation?'

'All of them highly medical, needless to say,' she said, relieved to have got away from the dangerous topics so easily.

'Them? Does that mean there's nobody special?'

'They would all consider themselves highly special!'

'But you don't?'

'I'm in no hurry to weed out any particular one from the rest,' she told him. Then, realising that she was losing an opportunity to reinforce the idea that she was not available, she added—entirely fictitiously, 'There is someone I might be prepared to feel more seriously about, but that will have to wait until I've sorted out my work situation.'

'What's he like?'

Curse the man and his persistence! Now she had to invent someone. She ran her mind quickly over the medical students and young doctors of her ac-quaintance, and found herself quite unable to pick out one from the mass and slot him into the role of im-aginary lover. They were all so much alike—hard-working, hard-playing, strangely schoolboyish, every one of them. It would have to be a matter of complete invention.

'He's older than me. Very tall and broad—but ab-solutely in proportion,' she fantasised, warming to the subject. 'He's fair, and his eyes are grey, and——' She broke off, hot under the collar as she realised that she was slipping into a description of Marcus himself.

'The ideal romantic hero,' he said drily.

'Not quite. He's got an attractive kink in his nose where it was broken once when he was playing rugby.' Marcus had a perfectly straight, almost Roman nose.

'Thank heaven for the broken nose,' he said, amused. 'The fellow was sounding too fictitiously perfect for words. And now what's amusing you?'

'Just the thought of——' she sought hurriedly for a name '—of Ambrose being considered perfect.'

'Ambrose?' Marcus said with mild disgust. 'Now he's got two handicaps.'

'You think so?' She deliberately made her voice dreamy. 'I rather like it.'

He fell silent again and stayed that way until they stopped for a mid-morning halt near Chalon.

Mistral drank thirstily when they opened up the box to refresh the horses, and again, while they each waited for the other to have coffee in the refreshment-room, they heard the dry cough, this time more frequently. When they drove on, Alex was as convinced as Marcus that all was not well with the little horse.

It grew hotter and hotter, and as she watched the kilometres flash by Alex shifted restlessly, trying to unstick her jeans from her legs. Her back, too, was still suffering a little from the fall she had had at the *abrivado*. Not that it troubled her for most of the time, but hours in the car tended to make her conscious of her bruises. Also she had unwisely left her sunglasses in her bag, and she had the beginnings of a bad headache.

Marcus surprised her by pulling off the road again at the refreshment area in the Forêt de Bligny.

'We'll eat now,' he said tersely. 'When we get to our night stop, I want to be free to get Mistral seen to.'

It was an unjoyful picnic, each of them preoccupied. Alex was beginning to wonder how much time would be

added on to their journey if they had to wait for a horse
to respond to treatment. She knew that they wouldn't
be allowed to take a sick animal across the Channel. Life
was getting more complicated by the minute.

The equestrian centre they were heading for proved
rather more difficult to find than last night's stopping
place, and by the time they reached it Alex's map-reading
was very much given the thumbs-down by an irritable
Marcus. When he came out of the long, low white house
after speaking to the head of the centre, however, he
looked somewhat relieved.

'We're in luck,' he said, getting back into the driving
seat. 'The vet's here at the moment, looking at one of
their horses with a damaged fetlock. As soon as he's
finished with that, he'll examine Mistral.'

'I'm so glad,' Alex said simply, and for the first time
in hours there was no hostility between them as he turned
to her.

'So am I. At least we'll know what it is, and whether
it's likely to be serious or not. It hasn't been the best of
days so far, has it?'

Alex felt a certain sympathy. 'As long as things aren't
serious, we can laugh about it all.'

But when Marcus and the vet stepped down from the
horse-box where they had left Mistral until she had been
examined, Marcus's face was grave. The vet headed for
the gate, and Marcus came over to where Alex was
stroking Lasco's neck.

'Strangles,' he said grimly, and her face instantly reflected the anxiety in his. Strangles was an unpleasant
and often dangerous equine illness involving fever and
throat abscesses. It could even be fatal.

'Oh, no!' she said.

'It's in the very early stages—we couldn't have caught
it much earlier, apparently—and he says Camargues are
pretty robust and resist it well, so that's encouraging.
He's given her a hefty shot of antibiotics, and I've got

to drive over to his place now to pick up more doses to give her—he didn't have enough on him of the right strength. We'll get her out and unhitch the box, then we'll leave the horses and get off quickly.'

'I could exercise Lasco while you do that. I don't suppose Mistral will have to be ridden until she responds to treatment, will she?' Alex said. It was not a purely unselfish suggestion. She couldn't bear the thought of getting into the Range Rover again.

Marcus rounded on her. 'For God's sake, how long does it take you to understand a simple fact? You are not going careering around an unknown area on your own. Not last night, not tonight, not tomorrow, not any time while you are in my employment. Are you determined to get lost or raped or murdered? What is it with you?'

'I understand, of course, that your chief worry is for your precious horse, but I actually thought I was making a helpful offer,' Alex said, her hackles rising.

'Don't imagine that you fool me for one instant. What you really mean is that you've had enough of being on the road in this temperature—correct?' he said scornfully, infuriating her by being absolutely right. 'Well, tough. We're not here for the fun of it. I don't want to drive any further either, but it has to be done.'

'Not by two of us. I have a splitting headache and I'm not getting in the car again.' She plumped herself down on the bank at the side of the field, glaring at him. 'You're being totally unreasonable. You can stop me going off on Lasco if you insist on making such a fuss, but at least I can stay here and see to feeding the horses. I'm not trying to get out of doing anything. And I'm sure the horses aren't going to go berserk and trample me to death,' she added nastily, 'if that happens to be the next item on your disaster fixation.'

He gave her a filthy look. 'The thing that puts any potential disaster on the agenda is your total failure to realise that there are sensible ways of behaving.'

She jumped to her feet again. 'You can't get much more sensible than going on a course to make sure you can deal with difficult situations. How many more times do I have to tell you I can take care of myself?'

'The "all girls together" self-defence classes?' The sneer in his voice fanned the flames.

'We had an instructor who was your size,' she countered swiftly.

'Who made sure that it all went like a ballet class, no doubt.'

Alex's temper finally broke the bounds of control. She almost danced around him in rage. 'All right, since you think you know it all. Try me out. Look—I'm turning my back on you. See how far you get if you make any attempt to grab me.'

'Don't be ridiculous. Pick a fight with someone your own size.'

'Afraid of losing your dignity, are you?' she flung over her shoulder at him. 'Or are you afraid that an eight-stone girl might manage to hurt you?'

'The reverse, actually,' he said coldly.

'Chicken! Coward!' she taunted.

He was standing there with folded arms, watching her looking both amazed and disgusted. Since she was well aware that she was going too far, but was too angry to back down, this only made her even more furious.

'The headache seems to have disappeared,' he told her coldly.

'They always do—when something that's a bigger pain than a headache turns up. Come on, be man enough to let me prove to you that you've been talking a load of rubbish. Look!' She brandished her arms in the air, her hair flying out as she circled him, her back towards him still. 'I'm not looking. Have the guts to have a go, at least. I can't make it much easier for you.'

'Very well, then, since you're hell-bent on making a fool of yourself.'

His sudden agreement made a stab of apprehension go through her, but she could do it! Hadn't she thrown her fifteen-stone instructor and been praised and made to demonstrate again for the class?

'Come on, then!' she called boldly.

'I'm coming.' His voice sounded nearer. 'And I'm going to talk myself towards you if you insist on standing with your back towards me. You shall at least have the benefit of knowing I'm on my way. Ten paces away from you now. And getting nearer... nearer...'

Alex tensed, every nerve ready and waiting. There were times when her hair and her temper blazed in tandem, and this was one of them. She would show him! She would silence him! Where the hell was he?

His hand touched her right arm, and she reacted instantly, snapping into a move that was going to demonstrate conclusively how wrong he had been to underrate her.

Instead, she found herself literally flying through the air to land on her back in a clump of deep grass and have every bit of breath knocked out of her.

Worse, without having seemed to move at all, Marcus was astride her, crouching down over her, his eyes blazing though his voice was steely and controlled.

'And how are you going to get out of this, you little fool?'

She had no breath to answer him, and no answer to give. And she was not only winded, but scared.

He stood up and stepped to one side, then reached for her hand and yanked her to her feet, where, to her shame, she was forced to cling on to him, bent over and fighting painfully for each breath.

He stood waiting for her to revive, his head turned to look down at her, watching her, infuriating her, until eventually she managed to get a couple of words out along with a nasty pinch of her fingers. 'Not fair!'

His lip curled. 'After the bravado, the whingeing. That figures. With an attitude like that, you'll live.' He freed himself from her grip. 'Now perhaps I can get on with the important business and withdraw from this ridiculous charade you cooked up.'

'You could have told me!' she choked again, but with more volume.

This time he smiled, a horrid, mocking smile. 'Next time you feel like getting yourself attacked, do yourself a favour. Make sure that you assailant doesn't know a bit more than you do.'

When he had driven off, she allowed herself to sink down and sit on the bank. The rotten man must be something like a black belt in judo, and he hadn't had the decency to tell her.

He had tossed her through the air like a sack of potatoes, the beast. And what exactly had you hoped to do to him? her conscience prodded maliciously. Oh! She drummed her heels on the bank in fury, then found that her headache had not gone at all, it had merely been overshadowed by her temper.

She sat there a little longer, feeling thoroughly sorry for herself and more than a little foolish, then got to her feet. She was not going to feed the horses. She didn't feel up to heaving anything around, not yet.

Through the trees, she saw the glint of water and it was like a beacon calling her. But Marcus Wakeford, the idiot, had gone off with her luggage, and therefore her bathing costume, in his wretched Range Rover, and lord alone knew how long he was going to be. Another wave of fury washed through her. Well, he was not going to stop her having a swim. She had skinny-dipped before, and she could do so now.

The water of the Armançon was like a healing balm. Alex didn't swim much; she let herself float near the bank for a while, then trod water, her eyes closed, just allowing herself to relax, unwind, and cool down. The sound of the water was gentle and hypnotic. She could almost allow herself to fall asleep.

'Ask what it would be least sensible for you to do, and I'm certain to know exactly what you're up to,' Marcus's voice said, giving her the shock of her life.

Alex panicked and choked on swallowed water, then made for the opposite bank where there were overhanging trees, swimming under water and only surfacing when she was at a safe distance.

She was just in time to see Marcus, stripped in no time, dive into the river and reappear halfway over.

'Keep away from me!' she called urgently.

He shook water from his head. 'Don't worry. I'm not thinking in terms of a repeat performance.'

'Why are you back so quickly?' she asked desperately.

'Because the vet only lives a couple of hundred yards along the road, as you would have found out if you hadn't leapt to the conclusion that it meant driving for miles.' He swam lazily to and fro, watching her. 'Why are you hanging around like Moses in the bulrushes?'

'I'm keeping my distance from you,' she snapped. 'Are you surprised?' He trod water, only seven or eight yards away from her, his fair hair strangely darkened and sleek.

'Don't overdramatise. I made sure you had the softest landing available. You're all right, I suppose?'

'No thanks to you.'

'I presume that you wouldn't have been foolish enough to swim if you had any ill effects from your—experience.'

'I'm not exactly being allowed to swim at the moment, am I?'

'A self-inflicted punishment. But don't worry. A quick dip was all I had in mind. I've had enough now. You would do well to come out too.'

He swam over to the bank and climbed out, his magnificent body—she was furious with herself for noticing—glistening as he stood looking across at her.

'Aren't you cold?' he called.

'Not in the least.' Alex struggled to control the chattering of her teeth. The river was fast-flowing and deep at this point, and in spite of the heat of the late afternoon she was by now chilled to the bone.

Marcus dried himself, taking his time. She swam to and fro, making sure to stay at the far side of the river, feeling shrivelled and icy.

'You really should come out now,' he called, still watching her with folded arms.

'Not yet.' She made her voice as pleasant as possible in the effort to get rid of him. 'Please don't wait.'

'No problem. There's no hurry to do anything else. But you really shouldn't stay in any longer. You'll regret it if you get too cold.'

Not half as much as I should regret getting out with you standing there watching, Alex thought grimly. Oh, what a fool she was! Who but an idiot would actually think she could get away with this sort of caper? Her temper would be her downfall—*was* her downfall at this very moment, if the wretched man didn't decide to go back to the field. She was going to have to tell him that she couldn't get out as long as he was standing there like a cross between a colossus and a guardian angel. She stopped swimming and looked over at him, wondering if her face was as blue as it felt to be, steeling herself to make her ridiculous confession.

He spoke first. 'This sun's glorious again after the water.' His face was turned up to the glowing sky. As she watched, he stretched his arms luxuriantly, then slowly lowered them, looking at her. 'Well, I suppose we could play this game for hours before you'd give in and be sensible.' She realised that a mocking smile was spreading across his face. 'If I turn my back, will that

solve your problem? I'll be gentleman enough to make
my towel available...' He kicked it to the edge of the
river. 'You haven't got one—or anything else the normal
person would consider necessary for a swim, of course—
since I had the luggage with me.'

He had known all the time, Alex thought furiously,
keeping a wary eye on his back as she swam over to the
bank and scrambled out, feeling hideously exposed, to
envelop herself in the damp beach towel he had 'made
available', as he put it. He had been deliberately mocking
her all the time. She pulled her jeans and shirt on, tugging
crossly as they dragged on her damp skin.

'I suppose this is your idea of the funniest joke in
Christendom,' she said venomously.

'Mildly amusing, agreed. Is it safe to turn round now?'
he asked politely. 'Or am I at risk from that temper of
yours again?'

'No. You're bigger than me. I've learned that lesson.'

'Good.' He turned and looked at her, and he wasn't
laughing now. 'I hope that makes two lessons well and
truly absorbed today. Power and privacy—never assume
you have either.' Then, without another word, he set off
and was back at the field ahead of her, no doubt pro-
pelled by sheer smugness, Alex told herself crossly.

Cool politeness ruled during the brief time they were
together setting up camp, then Marcus took Lasco off
for an evening ride, suggesting that Alex might like to
give Mistral a bit of gentle grooming. Both Mistral and
Alex found this soothing and beneficial, and by the time
Marcus came back she was able to speak to him without
iron bands of self-control round every word.

'I've been able to arrange for us to eat over at the
centre with the other guests,' he told her. 'It's been a
longer day today, and I don't think either of us feels like
hunting around for somewhere else in the area.'

Or having a *dîner à deux*, Alex thought, relieved.

They went across to the dining-room at eight-thirty, Alex welcoming the prospect of mixing with other people for a while. There were two other English families on holiday at the centre, Marcus had been told, and the two of them were to be put on a table for eight with their compatriots.

Who would recognise us from the rest of today's clashes? Alex thought. She was wearing her favourite leggings in a bold abstract print in peacock-blue and shades of green, with a white voile tunic. She had tied her hair back in the nape of her neck with a green ribbon, and put on the cluster earrings that picked out the colours of the leggings. With her feet in strappy sandals after the trainers that were the most practical wear for most of the journey, she felt quite festive, and very different from the either hot or cold bad-tempered shrew of earlier on.

Marcus too had returned from his bath with an air of simple, restrained elegance in a fine oatmeal cotton sweater and sage gabardine trousers. As he drew out her chair in the beamed dining-room and smilingly waited for her to sit down, the light from the wall-lamp gleaming on his hair, no one would have recognised the sarcastic, irritating creature who had so annoyed her.

The two English families—an older couple from the Midlands, and a young couple from Essex with two children—were good company, and the meal was excellent. Alex couldn't help noticing how quickly the children took to Marcus, and how good he was with them. They dragged him away at the end of the meal to see the ponies they considered 'theirs', but she observed with interest that he did not allow the little boy and girl to do anything or go anywhere he felt the owners of the riding centre would not approve. With them he had a natural, pleasant authority which the children obeyed without question. So it was only family that he spoiled rotten, Alex noted. Everyone else was kept firmly in place, including her—or so he thought. But, she reflected with secret satisfaction, he didn't know who she was. In that respect, she had the upper hand.

The day, though, all in all, had ended far better than it had run for most of the time. As Mistral was given her last injection of the day, Alex, holding the torch, watched Marcus's caring expression, and was forced to wonder fleetingly if a man who cared for animals could be all bad. They prepared for bed in the darkness in an atmosphere relatively neutral. Marcus even demonstrated the art of taming the hammock. But before she got in he put a slim tube in her hand.

'Put this on those bruises of yours,' he said, showing that he had not merely surmised that she was swimming naked earlier on, he had actually seen. Alex was thankful for the darkness. 'I had no idea you'd had such a rough tumble at the *abrivado*,' he went on. 'You should have told me.'

Alex did her best to ignore the embarrassing side of the situation. 'It's nothing,' she said. 'I bruise easily— mine is that kind of skin. But thanks, anyway.'

He shook his head as he looked at her. 'You ridiculous girl...' he said, and it sounded almost like an endearment. She felt her heartbeat quicken.

Then there was a sudden beat of wings and a flash of white only a foot or two over their heads, and Alex jumped nervously.

'It's only an owl,' he said, as they both watched the hunter disappear into the darkness.

An owl, or an omen... Alex wondered. The timing of its flight and its no doubt deadly purpose seemed to speak to her of danger. Danger that stayed in her mind as she said a quick goodnight and got into her hammock. Despite the anger of the day, and despite all her defiant thoughts and behaviour, when Marcus's voice had softened as he spoke, she had again felt a wave of the yearning, resolution-destroying weakness that had swept over her at his touch the night before.

The owl could not have timed things better. She snuggled down in her sleeping-bag, staring up into the star-studded blackness of the sky, and forced herself to think through the day, rewriting the script of it. Several times, on the quiet, she had taken out the little black purse and looked at it with pleasure. Such behaviour turned sour in her mind now. It had more than a touch of Judas about it. How could she possibly feel gratitude, let alone attraction, towards the man who had created such havoc in her family's life? She had always thought of herself as the sensible one with Elaine the vulnerable, foolish sister.

Now she was not sure. She was going to have to watch herself—not be certain of anything, whether it be love or hatred. Love could be betrayed, for hadn't she found herself coming close to embarking on the path that could lead to betrayal of Elaine and her father? How she hated herself for that now. But what price hatred? Hatred could melt at the tone of a voice.

She turned her back on Marcus, and waited soberly for sleep to envelop her and blot out the depressingly unsatisfactory image of herself she was left with. Memories of accusing school reports floated through her mind. Must do better... Must do better...

CHAPTER FIVE

IF THINGS had seemed bad last night, fate stepped in and made them decidedly worse just before their morning departure.

Alex had remembered her watch, which was in her soft case, and was keeping Marcus waiting while she fumbled through her clothes to find it. In her haste to end the delay, she threw the unzipped bag back into the hatchback, where it rebounded and fell out, spilling its contents on to the ground. As quickly as that, disasters could happen.

Alex rushed forward to pick things up, her first thoughts being that she didn't fancy her personal items of clothing being handled by Marcus, but then she saw him reach for a little maroon book, and her heart gave a frightening lurch. It was her passport—and inside it was her full, her real name.

'I'll take that!' she said hurriedly.

He stood up, holding it out of her reach. 'Why so fast? Afraid I might see the full horrors of your passport photograph?'

'No!' She tried to snatch it from him without any success. 'Please don't look. It's a horrible photograph!' she pleaded, her heart racing like a wild thing.

'They always are. That's what makes for entertainment.'

He opened the passport, and looked at the photograph, then at her. 'What a fuss about nothing. It's quite a decent one. No fun at all.'

For a second, a desperately hopeful second, she thought she was going to get away with it. But then she saw his eyes go to the opposite page. 'No mention of distinguishing marks now, otherwise I might, at this very moment, be on the point of discovering——'

He stopped, and Alex knew that her game was up. He had seen her name. He must have done. What else could the sudden silence mean? Nothing short of a miracle could stop him putting two and two together now. She crouched down, blindly picking up clothes any old how and stuffing them into her bag. As of this moment, she was in trouble—serious trouble.

The silence seemed to go on forever. Then at last he spoke.

'Ever get called Sandie?' she heard him ask with deadly slowness, his voice cold but oh, so full of meaning.

Weak with dread, she left her bag on the ground and stood up to face him. 'I once was...' she said faintly.

'I rather thought you might have been. Don't tell me—that would be at the time when your surname was different too, wouldn't it? Not plain Ward, but Leeward. Sandie Leeward. Right?'

She nodded, her heart in her mouth, almost paralysed by the look on his face.

'And something tells me you're not the only young Miss Leeward. You have a sister. Right?'

She swallowed hard. 'Let's not play games, Marcus. It's obvious that you know I'm Elaine's sister.'

'But the knowledge is so recent,' he said with cold mockery. 'You must allow a little time for me to absorb it. Perhaps we should begin by the first honest greeting that has taken place between us.' He held out a hand towards her, rock-steady while hers was trembling furiously. But the rigid muscles of his face were evidence of how angry he was. 'How do you do, Sandie Leeward?'

She was so shocked by the sudden collapse of her carefully maintained deception that she blindly stretched out her hand towards his. Instead of receiving a mocking handshake, though, she was pulled roughly towards him, her hand rejected and her shoulders gripped as he stuck his face within inches of hers, his features contorted with fury.

'Explanation time.' His voice was icy. 'Why the undercover act? Ashamed of your name, are you?'

'No.' Alex's head lifted proudly. 'Never.' She drew on all her courage and looked him straight in the eye for the first time since he had seen her passport. 'But I thought a Wakeford might not find it palatable.'

He looked scornfully at her. 'Don't hide behind your forebears.'

'I'm not doing so. The present generation has given ample ground for wariness.'

He pushed her roughly away from him. 'What a self-interested, scheming bitch you are.'

'That's unfair. To qualify for that description I would have had to know who you were in advance. And believe me,' she said venomously, 'if I had known that, no circumstance, however difficult, would have made me come to you.'

After a moment he said, 'How come you were so certain that I was the man who had known your dear sister?'

'Your name—which Liz hadn't known in full.'

'Names are not unique.'

'And Elaine had shown me your photograph.'

'A pity she wasn't moved to show me yours.' His voice was taut with venom.

'There you are, then,' she said simply. 'You don't need any further explanation of why I didn't feel inclined to use my real name. You wouldn't have entertained the idea of travelling away from hell with me, let alone back to England, would you?'

'Whereas you, on the other hand, were so desperate for a free ride that you'd stoop to any measure to get it.'

Alex's face lost its pallor as a wave of colour swept up her cheeks. 'If you remember, I tried to leave once I knew who you were. I was as bowled over then as you are now.'

'Bowled over? I'm plain angry,' he said fiercely.

'Well, whatever you want to call it. I had to think on the spot, and it wasn't easy.' She kicked at a tuft of grass. 'I wish you'd never come after me that day. I'd have muddled through somehow. Don't think I've enjoyed the past two days.'

'The fact of who you are certainly casts light on the switching from friendliness to high horse.'

Alex's lip curled scornfully. 'I suppose you think every woman should fling herself at you and say "Yes, please!" as soon as you crook your little finger.'

'I mean that it struck me as odd that such heavy weather should be made of a meaningless kiss.'

'Well, now you know,' she said curtly. 'I'm Elaine's sister. That's something I am capable of forgetting for a misguided second under the influence of moonlight and wine, but not in the cold light of day.'

'How very commendable,' he sneered. 'But I'm forgetting the social niceties. Tell me, how is your dear sister?'

Alex's eyes flashed emerald fire in reaction to the sarcasm in his voice. 'She's married, she has a delightful baby, and she's very happy indeed.'

'I'm so glad to hear that. Success at last, after one failed marriage and one failed relationship. It appears that the old saying is true—third time lucky.'

'How can you *say* something so rude and callous?' she fired at him.

'How can you *do* what you have done?' he retorted equally quickly. 'But you don't have to answer that one, do you? The answer sticks out a mile to someone who got to know your sister in the circumstances of my meeting with her. It's obvious that the art of deception runs in the family.'

Alex crouched down again and finished stuffing her things back into her bag, then stood up to face him. 'Well, there's nothing to be gained by raking over the past. I presume you'd like me to make myself scarce as quickly as possible. Unfortunately in order to do that I shall have to ask you to lend me some money. You can imagine how little I like doing that, but it seems the most simple way out of an unpleasant situation for both of us.'

'Turn tail and run? Is that another family characteristic you share with your sister?'

'You're despicable!'

'And you're forgetting something.'

'But I'm sure you'll tell me what it is.' She looked balefully at him.

'You happen to have entered into an agreement with me. Nothing has changed. I still have two horses to get back to England. I still need help with them. Are you telling me that you intend backing out now that your little deception has been uncovered?'

Now it was Alex's turn to be dumbfounded. She stared at him for a silent second. 'Are you saying that you'll still go along with having me with you?'

'It's amazing what one can go along with when it's a matter of convenience,' he said unpleasantly.

'I—I don't know how it could possibly work.'

'If you're talking about relationships, nor do I. But, as far as the job in hand is concerned, we grit our teeth and get on with it. Nobody says we have to enjoy ourselves. And, judging by your performance so far, you'll find it a relief to be able to be absolutely open about your own dissatisfaction with the situation.'

'This is one hell of a mess,' Alex said fervently.

'I fully agree—but the longer we hang around, the longer we shall have to endure it. You chose to work for me, so I say we get the show on the road.'

He left her to stow her own bag in the back of the Range Rover and join him in front. Alex felt terrible at the thought of the day ahead. More terrible when she faced up to the thought that it might be more than one day—far more.

'If only I'd known——' she began when the silence became intolerable.

'Do me a favour,' he said curtly. 'Just don't say anything. Keep it all to yourself—suppositions, thoughts, apologies—the lot.'

'I have nothing to apologise for,' she said stiffly.

'I'm sure you don't for a moment think you have. As with your sister, self-interest takes precedence over all else.'

Alex rounded on him in the close confines of the Range Rover. 'I think we'd better leave my sister out of it.'

'Well out of it,' he said with studied offensiveness. 'When she runs, she runs. Right into the Technicolor world of the American dream, from what you've said.'

His voice was so vicious as he said this that Alex knew there was nothing to be gained from arguing. He was arrogant, unfair, and—in view of his treatment of Elaine—totally unreasonable. But there was no point in battling against prejudice. Better to keep quiet.

It was certainly a far from easy day. Communication between them was kept to an absolute minimum apart from a terse announcement from Marcus that they would be staying that night with friends of his in a small château in the Forêt de Lyons. Shortly after they entered the beautiful beech forest, he pulled the Range Rover over to the side of the road and stopped.

'We're not there yet. We have to get something clear before we arrive,' he said.

Alex waited warily.

At last he went on. 'I think it's possible—perhaps even likely—that we will have to stay a day or two with Tim and Christiane, since both horses will have to be passed by a vet at Dieppe and a delay with friends will be far preferable to one at the port.'

'I realise that,' Alex said quietly.

'Of course. You're the young lady who knows it all, aren't you?' he gave her a look full of sarcasm.

'Not quite all.' Her voice was strained. 'I don't have a clue, for instance, how we're going to get through the journey in this kind of atmosphere.'

'Exactly. That is precisely why I've stopped. If we are forced to accept Tim and Christiane's hospitality, the least we can do is behave in a civilised manner. That means pretending like hell that we can tolerate each other. Even enjoy each other's company. Otherwise we're going to make life damned embarrassing and awkward for some very nice people.'

'I expect I can manage that,' Alex said wearily.

'Do you? Of course—you've had a couple of days' dress rehearsal. I'm blowed if I know whether I'm a good enough actor to pull it off.'

She was so fed up by now that she felt the sting of tears, but not for the world would she let him see how badly his attitude was affecting her. It was so easy to dislike someone, she thought miserably, and so terribly hard to accept being disliked in return.

'However——' he slapped the steering-wheel '—courtesy demands that we at least make the effort. So, to fill you in a little, Tim is English, Christiane French. He has rather more money than he knows what to do with, but instead of rushing around trying to amuse himself he has bought this decrepit château which no one else would touch with a barge-pole, and together he and Christiane are bringing it back to life. They can't have children, but other people's children gravitate towards them like filings to a magnet, as do friends and relations. They are two of the nicest people I know, and I don't want anything to upset them. Is that clear?'

'Perfectly. I hope they will have no cause to regret my presence.'

'You'd better do more than hope.'

He threw the car viciously into gear again and they moved off through the dappled green light of the forest.

The Château Ibert seemed to grow from and blend with the land. Ivy climbed up its rose-beige stone walls, binding them to the ground from which the green leaves grew. The walls themselves laid their shimmering reflection over the waters of the moat, and the beech forest cradled the whole in a clearing of the forest. Alex thought she had never seen a lovelier place and even Marcus was moved to speak about it.

'Before Tim and Christiane got at the Château,' he said in a voice that was halfway to normal, 'most of the walls were in the moat, and there wasn't a single habitable room in the place. They had a fleet of caravans for workmen, friends and helpers—and themselves—for the first year. That was five years ago. It's miraculous what they've achieved since. There's Tim.'

A lean, dark, intelligent-looking man was getting off a ride-on mower with which he had been cutting the grass between the moat and the trees. He came over towards them, and Marcus jumped down.

'So you made it, and on schedule. Well done!' He and Marcus shook hands warmly, then Tim turned the first pleasant smile she had seen in hours on Alex. 'And who is this?' he asked. 'Do your stuff, Marcus.'

'Alex is helping me with the horses on the journey. Alex Leeward...otherwise known as Sandie,' Marcus said, the malice returning to his steely eyes as he looked at Alex. 'Timothy Hughes, an old schoolfriend of mine.'

'Hello, Sandie. Nice to meet you.' Tim gave Alex a warm handshake.

'Hello—but I'm afraid none of my friends calls me Sandie these days. I'm Alex to everyone who counts.' And let that find the spot, Marcus Wakeford, she thought.

'Alex it is. So it sounds as though you two go back quite a way.' Tim looked at them both with interest.

'You could say we have a bit of history behind us,' Marcus said coolly. He looked around. 'Well—where is everybody? Not running the place on your own, are you?'

'No—there's the usual mixed bunch here, but plenty of room for all. Christiane's cousin and her husband and children from Nantes are with us, but only until tomorrow. Jean-Paul—that's Christiane's brother,' he added in explanation for Alex, 'will be staying on for another week. They've all gone off to Rouen for the afternoon but instructions have been left with Albertine about rooms. If you drive through the courtyard to the stables, Marcus, you can point Alex towards the kitchen and Albertine, then go on through to the stables and I'll meet you there. I'm looking forward to seeing these beasts you've been lugging around.'

'There's a bit of a story about them, but I'll tell you later,' Marcus said, getting back into the Range Rover.

As they drove over the bridge and into the courtyard, he said to Alex in the tone reserved for her in private, 'First hurdle over. At least we have company. That should sugar the pill.'

'Yes. It was a great relief to hear that,' she said equally coldly.

He paused long enough to introduce Albertine, who came out to meet them wiping her floury arms on a towel, then left Alex with the housekeeper, saying he would bring over the luggage later.

Albertine, a smiling woman of advanced middle age, had the matter-of-fact, down-to-earth approach to relationships that Alex had often encountered in rural areas. Her awkward English increased the blunt impression given by her first question.

'*Alors—madame* said me ask. You and Monsieur Mark—you are lovers or friends?'

'Neither,' Alex said, colouring. 'Employer and employee, actually.' She remembered Marcus's barbed reference to their history. 'Though we did know each other a little before this journey,' she added.

'*Bon.* So you wish two bedrooms?' Albertine said.

'Definitely!' Alex agreed with emphasis that made the Frenchwoman smile.

The room into which Alex was shown was at the back of the Château, and presumably overlooked the stable yard, because she could hear Marcus and Tim down below.

Albertine demonstrated the hanging space in the beautifully carved yew wardrobe, pointed out towels on the old-fashioned free-standing towel rail, and busily turned back a corner of the white embroidered bedcover. Finally she threw open the shutters to let sunlight in on the warm autumn colours of the magnificent antique Indian carpet, then with the words, 'Is more, you ask, please!' she went back downstairs.

Alex closed the door and sat on a carved, high-backed chair, bemused, and still suffering from the odd sensation of unrolling road before the eyes that long journeys often left her with. How good it was to have her own space. She suspected that she was going to need it. Marcus might talk of behaving as though they got on well, but he had made sure so far that there had been several stings in the tails of his apparently pleasant words—just for her.

When he knocked on her door a few minutes later and handed over her bags, grim-faced, she turned down the passed-on offer of a cup of tea, and, saying she was tired, told him that she preferred to have a restful bath before dinner. He reminded her again to put on a pleasant front, then without another word he turned and left.

After her bath, Alex lay on her bed for a while thinking about the situation in which she found herself. She hated it. Although the unpleasant aspect of it originated in the business between Marcus and Elaine, so much of the blame seemed attributed to herself at the moment. When she had first met Marcus, he had been justifiably piqued by the Liz business, but—in spite of who she knew him to be—tolerable company. She thought of the picnic lunch at the *abrivado*, her first meeting with Mistral and Lasco, the meal out in the Vercors... But now the knowledge of who she was had turned him into a thoroughly unpleasant, vicious creature who couldn't look at her without giving the impression that he found her supremely distasteful.

She dressed for courage in a lime-green loose silk tunic and narrow black trousers in the same soft fabric, her hair tied back with a matching lime and black striped scarf, and slim ballet pumps on her feet.

Her heart sank as she opened her bedroom door to go down and thought of the prospect of facing up to Marcus's hostile eyes again. Battleship-grey, they seemed to be now, every time he turned them on her.

In the event there was nothing to dread. Tim, not Marcus, rose and came over to greet her and take her on a conducted tour of the others already gathered on the west terrace.

Christiane was a petite brunette with big brown eyes and a mobile, witty face. She welcomed Alex warmly and asked if she had everything she wanted, in every way the perfect, easy hostess. Rémy, Christiane's cousin, explained in competent English that his wife was still upstairs getting the two girls ready for bed before

bringing them down for dinner. Then Tim introduced
Christiane's younger brother, Jean-Paul.

Jean-Paul had double his ration of charm, Alex decided as he urged her to try a glass of Beaumes de Venise
and took her over to the drinks trolley. He was dark,
like Christiane, and had eyes that looked uncritically—
even appreciatively—at Alex. The change was welcome.
He told her that he worked for a multinational company
and spent a considerable amount of time at the British
offices. Since Tim, Marcus and Christiane were deep in
reminiscences which he said meant as little to him as to
her, he suggested a walk round the grounds, and Alex
was nothing loath to get away from the vicinity of
Marcus. Rémy, invited to go with them, said he had
walked more than enough for one day, and sprawled
comfortably in a garden chair.

When they came back from their brief walk, Marcus
had time to say under his breath as Alex passed by him,
'You've got over your tiredness, I see.'

'Yes,' Alex said, smiling sweetly. 'It's surprising how
refreshing pleasant company can be.'

Further *sotto voce* acid exchanges were prevented as
Rémy's wife Thérèse came up with the children to say
hello, and almost at the same time Christiane called, '*A
table, tout le monde.*' There was a general milling around
of people that separated Alex from Marcus once again
and she found herself sitting next to Jean-Paul at the
table on the terrace, with Marcus not quite opposite her
on the other side.

Conversation switched between French for the sake
of the little girls and English, which all the adults spoke
competently. The talk was lively, and Alex found herself
relaxing.

They had reached the cheese stage when Christiane
leaned forward so that she could see Alex, and with a
teasing glance at Marcus said, 'Tell me, Alex, what is
your opinion of a man who thinks nothing of travelling

all the way to the Camargue just to buy two horses? Don't you think him rather extravagant?'

Marcus's grey eyes were watching her coolly. I must say nothing to show that I think his wife is pampered and his daughter spoiled, Alex thought swiftly.

'I think it shows how very much he cares for his wife and family,' she said.

There was a puzzled silence, then eyes turned on Marcus.

'Marcus, what have you been telling this girl?' Christiane asked.

'Nothing, truly.' He picked up his wine glass and drank from it, watching Alex over its rim. 'I'm afraid she has a tendency to jump to conclusions. I merely let her keep her assumption that I had a pampered, demanding woman driving me on to indulge her.'

The outbreak of good-humoured remonstrance gave Alex time to get over her surprise and embarrassment, and she waited for the noise to die down before saying across the table, 'So you're self-indulgent, not indulging of others, then, Marcus?'

A burst of laughter greeted this, and Jean-Paul murmured a soft, 'Bravo!' under cover of the general amusement at Marcus's expense.

As far as everyone else was concerned, Marcus took it well, laughing with the rest. But Alex felt him watching her as the meal went on, and she knew that his surface pleasantness concealed something else that she could read only too easily in the depths of his eyes when they met hers. She concentrated on Jean-Paul, who made it very pleasant indeed for her to do so.

'How well do you know this part of France?' he asked her.

'Hardly at all,' Alex told him. 'I've spent holidays in Brittany, and down in the South, but Normandy is part of the great unknown, I'm afraid.'

'Then we must remedy that,' he said charmingly, going on to list the attractions of the area. 'Perhaps you would like a drive through the forest before darkness falls?' he suggested. 'I know you have spent a lot of the day on the road, but a leisurely run through the trees with the roof of the car open and the wind in your hair—glorious hair, I must say——' He broke off to twist a shining dark copper strand round his slim brown finger, giving it a gentle, teasing tug, then concluded, 'That would be far more *agréable, tu ne penses pas?*'

Alex saw that Marcus had noted both the gesture and the intimate form of address, and felt a flash of pleasure that another man should so obviously find her attractive. It applied balm to the hurt of being so undisguisedly hated by a Wakeford.

'That sounds a lovely idea,' she said with real appreciation.

'Then leave it to me.'

With total assurance that nothing and no one would stand in the way of what he wanted to do, Jean-Paul called across to Marcus, 'Marcus, *mon vieux*, you don't mind if I take Alex away for a little while, do you? I want to seize the opportunity to introduce her to our lovely beech forest.'

Marcus answered smoothly, so smoothly that only Alex knew the venom underlying his words. 'What a nice idea. But I'm sorry—Alex and I have work to do. I want the horses groomed and settled.' His eyes rested on Alex. 'She may deceive you by looking decorative, but I'm afraid she's a working girl.'

'What a taskmaster you are, Marcus. But even working girls are allowed some leisure. We shall have to postpone our outing until then,' Jean-Paul said, amiably enough. When Marcus's attention was drawn elsewhere, though, he said softly to Alex, 'Is this man jealous of my attentions to his working girl, do you think, *ma chère* Alex?'

'Absolutely not!' Alex said hurriedly.

'Then if not jealous, he is very disagreeable,' Jean-Paul told her. 'He shall not prevent our little excursion. Tomorrow, when there are no annoying attentions to be paid to his precious horses, we shall escape. You agree?'

'I'm sure that will be possible. And I'd like it very much.' Marcus's baleful eye turned on her again. 'And now I'd better go and change,' she said hurriedly. 'This is hardly the right gear for working with four-legged animals.'

'Indeed not,' Jean-Paul said, rising with her, and whispering in her ear as he drew out her chair, 'But it's absolutely right for pleasing the two-legged variety.'

She laughed at him, then excused herself and went up to change.

Once she was away from the others, she could give full rein to her feelings about Marcus. After all his pious talk of not embarrassing his friends, how much effort had he made to ensure that all went smoothly? Damn all, if the truth were told. She smarted with annoyance at the way he had deliberately tried to make her look a fool at the dinner-table, feeling only slight consolation at the way she had managed to turn the tables on him.

As for this cock-and-bull story about the horses having to be groomed—that was pure malice. He had thought there was a chance that she might actually spend a pleasant hour or so with Jean-Paul, and he'd stepped right in and thrown cold water on the idea.

On a wave of anger, she pulled on her jeans and shirt again, and made her way to the stables. Marcus wasn't there, and she buried her face in Mistral's neck, letting warm animal therapy melt the knot of rage inside her, then sighed and set to work with the curry comb.

She didn't look up when she heard Marcus come into the stables, expecting him to go straight into Lasco's stall, but instead he appeared at her side.

'I'll give Mistral her injection if you can break off a second,' he said curtly.

Alex stepped back without speaking.

In silence he dealt swiftly and skilfully with the horse's medication, but when he turned round his eyes met hers.

'Feeling hard done by?' he asked sarcastically.

'Certainly not.' She resumed the grooming.

'Nothing bugging you at all, then?'

'Nothing worth wasting time on.'

He put a hand in the path of her grooming. 'I'm buying your time. I decide what constitutes a waste of it.'

She straightened up again. 'I think you established beyond all reasonable doubt that you're the boss,' she said, her tone as scathing as his. 'Who could doubt it after this evening?'

He folded his arms and stared at her, a glint of satisfaction in steely grey eyes. 'So I was right. You are peeved because your fun-time with Jean-Paul didn't materialise.'

'You have every right to decide exactly when the horses should be groomed—even if they were both thoroughly attended to only this morning,' she said in a voice straight from the North Pole. 'But the thing I certainly do take exception to is the way you maintained a pretence of being married until you could embarrass me in public. Do you really think that was necessary?'

'About as necessary as it was for you to jump to the conclusion that a wife existed. I was rather tired of your assumptions by that time.' He ticked them off. 'I would employ you at the drop of a hat——'

'That thought didn't last long,' Alex interjected.

'I would turn you down because you had the gumption to remove your weight from a startled, rearing horse,' he went on, ignoring the interruption, 'and then the peach of them all: I had a demanding wife. I let that one stand. My imaginary married status perhaps made you feel safer.'

'Or you.' Alex looked scornfully at him. 'Though you can hardly have been under the misapprehension that I was going to fling myself at you.'

He gave an unpleasant smile. 'Apart from your nude cavorting in the Armançon. I did wonder at that point. But that turned out to be stupidity, not scheming.'

Alex coloured, just about hanging on to the reins of her temper.

'I can see now, looking back with the benefit of hindsight, that you never actually said anything about the wife I thought you had. You had much more to say on the subject of Rebecca. Just to get the record quite correct, she does exist?'

His face darkened. 'You know damned well Rebecca exists. Don't play games on that subject.'

'Are you the only one allowed to play games, then?' Alex retorted. 'If your marital status is a myth, don't blame me for questioning your fatherhood as well.'

'I have never claimed fatherhood. If you want me to spell it out unnecessarily, I will. Rebecca is my brother's child. Her parents are both dead, so to all intents and purposes she is mine.' He watched her through narrowed eyes. 'And I don't think a little indulgence is out of place, in the circumstances.'

'Not if you imagine material gifts can make up for what she's lost,' Alex said scornfully.

He grabbed her shoulders and almost lifted her off the ground as his features contorted with anger.

'I was telling you, not asking your opinion,' he snarled. 'Always ready with the smart answer, aren't you Miss Know-it-all? Some day some man's going to shut you up like this!'

And before she could utter a squeak he had crushed her mouth under his own. In the initial seconds of blistering resentment, Alex knew exactly what he was doing. He was trying to settle with despicable male dominance a situation which was not resolving itself as easily as he wished, and for one wild, struggling moment she attempted to fight him off. But what started with anger suddenly took on its own momentum and direction. Abuse fused into an explosion of white-hot passion. Alex's hands had jerked up to beat against him, but only once, after which they were frozen in shock against the warmth of his shoulders as he broke off and held her away to stare with heated bewilderment into her own dazed eyes. Neither of them seemed to move, but then he was kissing her again—a different kind of kiss—her hands were of their own volition beginning to slide round his neck, and she didn't know whether her smothered no had meant, Don't do this, or Don't stop doing it. All she knew was that will and sense and independence seemed to have deserted her, and when he let her go she was as weak as a kitten.

'Pity I won't be around to tell the poor blighter how quickly he can settle your hash,' he said, and now she could see only contempt in his eyes.

Again! It happened again! Alex thought desperately. I forgot Elaine, my father, everything... She looked at his unrelenting hostile face, and the thought that all that wild, uncontrollable emotion might have stemmed only from herself appalled her. What kind of woman was she, that she could sink under such a riot of feelings for any man, let alone this particular one whom there was all the reason in the world to hate? She crouched down and began feverishly to gather together all the grooming equipment.

'In a sudden hurry, aren't you?' he asked.

'I'm putting these things away,' she said, with what self-possession she could muster, not looking at him. 'I have no intention of staying in here with you. I'll come down early tomorrow morning and do it when there's less chance of interruption.'

She made for the door, but he barred her way for a moment.

'You can't go in yet. You're supposed to be working, remember? If you're still seething because you've missed a bit of dalliance with a smart-arsed Frenchman, I'll ferry you around the Forêt de Lyons myself.'

The contrast between his unconcealed contempt and the feelings that had just raged through her during that travesty—on his part—of a kiss refuelled enough of her anger to enable her to look him in the eye again.

'I'd sooner you jumped in the moat,' she said, choking on the words. Then, blindly, she ducked under his arm to escape to her room.

CHAPTER SIX

CHRISTIANE appeared in the stables just as Alex was finishing cleaning the tack next day.

'O-o-h!' she said, giving the vowel a very French sympathetic sound. 'The poor girl! She is forced to work day and night by this monster of a Marcus!'

Alex smiled. 'Not really. I'm only finishing off what didn't get done last night.'

Christiane hung around, chatting, until the tack was finished, then slipped her arm through Alex's as they walked round and back towards the main entrance.

'You must not take him too seriously, this man who plays tricks on you at the dinner-table. He might act like a great cross bear, but inside there is another Marcus who is really quite nice, believe it or not.'

Alex made some non-committal answer, but felt that she knew Marcus far better than Christiane did.

When they reached the dining-room he was there, waiting for breakfast, looking decidedly military in khaki shirt and trousers, with the sun glinting on his immaculate fair head. Ready for battle again? Alex wondered warily. He kissed Christiane on both cheeks, and even managed a, 'Morning!' in Alex's direction, but his eyes moved quickly away from hers.

Christiane went off to the kitchen, leaving the two of them together.

'How was Mistral this morning?' Marcus asked coolly.

'I thought she seemed rather better.'

'Then we'll give her a little gentle exercise. Lasco certainly needs it, and the ground is easy enough around here. Coffee?'

Alex held out her big blue and white cup, knowing that his civility was meaningless, a front for the rest of the household, and feeling far from calm about the prospect of a ride alone with him. Christiane came back with a basket of croissants fresh from the oven, and her sunny presence took care of the rest of the time spent in the house. No one else appeared, and when they had finished eating Marcus and Alex went straight back to the stables.

The little horse seemed glad to be out and about, walking happily in Lasco's footsteps. It wasn't necessary to talk as they followed the quiet paths through the forest. Birdsong and dancing, dappled sunlight prevented the atmosphere from seeming unbearably heavy, and they returned to the stables with hardly a word exchanged.

It was Marcus who eventually broke the silence as they were hanging up the saddles.

'I see you cleaned the tack,' he said.

'I said I would.'

'Forgive me for not readily assuming that saying and doing were linked in your family.' He gave Mistral's flank a congratulatory pat, not allowing Alex time for a retort. 'At least she stood up to the ride well. That's something to be thankful for.'

'She found it more pleasant than I did,' she told him coldly.

'Then you'll be gratified to hear that I intend spending no more time in your presence today. Tim has asked me to go and have a look at some restoration work on a place about the same age as his beloved Château Ibert. We'll be gone most of the day. No doubt you're capable of finding something to do.'

A devil got into Alex. 'A free day?' she asked casually.

'Now that this bit's over, yes.'

'In that case, I'll probably take up the kind offer Jean-Paul made last night,' she said. Jean-Paul whom you described so charmingly as a smart-arsed Frenchman, remember? she added mentally, giving a covert glance in Marcus's direction. His face had taken on a thunderous look.

'Jean-Paul may have other things to do,' he said coldly.

'If he has, I'm sure he will say so. But last night he seemed very anxious to make sure that I would be given the promised tour at some time that didn't conflict with my work for you. From what you've said, it sounds as though today would be appropriate.'

'As long as you don't make too much of a nuisance of yourself,' he said nastily. She left the stables quickly. Something hit the inside of the stable door with a resounding whack before she had gone more than a few paces. Alex felt a certain vicious satisfaction. If he had thrown something in temper, she hoped it had rebounded and hit him.

She sought out Christiane who said that Jean-Paul had not yet shown his face, but she was about to take him coffee and would tell him that Alex wanted to speak to him.

Jean-Paul came knocking at her bedroom door while she was fresh from her shower and still wearing the silk kimono Christiane had thoughtfully provided. He leaned against the doorpost, his eyes taking in every inch of her.

'*Charmante*!' was his first word, quickly followed by a kiss on both cheeks. 'In France, we salute each other like this,' he said, his expression wicked.

'Do you indeed?' she asked sceptically. 'I thought this was the land of the handshake.'

'We do other things with hands.' He seized one of hers and brought it swiftly to his lips, his eyes sparkling with such roguishness that it was impossible to be cross with him.

'I expect you had some other purpose in knocking on my door,' Alex said patiently. 'I hardly think you're here

because you suddenly felt an urge to demonstrate a
hundred different ways of greeting.'

'Of course. Christiane informs me that you wish to
see me. You are not going to ask me to come in?'

'In England we never invite strange men into our
bedrooms.'

He laughed and expressed disbelief. 'What—never?'

'Well, hardly ever. And certainly not if they happen
to be outrageous Frenchmen.'

'How strange you English are! Never mind, I shall
not hold it against you.' He straightened up. 'So! We
are to be allowed to escape today? Marcus has had a
change of heart?'

'Well . . . he's given me a free day.'

'I am delighted. He had—what do you say?—slept on
it.'

'He must have done.'

'And what would you like to do today?'

'Anything you suggest.'

'O-oh!' He cast his eyes heavenwards and gave the
vowel the same expressive sound Christiane had invested
it with. 'She plays a game of chance, this girl!'

Alex gave him a firm look. 'Anything you suggest from
the local tourist schedule was what I meant. You said
you would show me Normandy. That's what I'd like you
to do.'

'Then that is what we shall do—and I promise you a
delightful time. *Un quart d'heure*? Just time for me to
have a bowl of coffee?'

'I'll be ready,' Alex said.

She had momentary doubts about what a man who
came on so strong at the start of a day would be like at
the end of it, but shook them off. Ten minutes later she
was ready, wearing a pale apricot Swiss cotton dress,
gold tassel earrings and discreet touches of both make-
up and White Linen perfume.

The last thing she wanted to do was bump into Marcus as she went downstairs, but that was exactly what happened. He stopped, blocking her way, and eyed her belligerently, taking in every detail of her appearance.

'I take it from the finery that the outing's on?'

'Was there something more you wanted me to do?' Alex asked politely.

'It's a good job there isn't with you done up like a dog's dinner.'

Alex kept a tight rein on her temper while he stood in her path, fulminating.

'Well—if there's nothing more, I'll wish you a good day,' she told him, beginning to edge sideways past him.

With a brusque movement he seized her arm and quickly turned her back up the stairs.

'Not so fast. I want a private word before you go,' he said as he opened the door of her room and went in with her, closing the door behind them.

'It's a good job Jean-Paul didn't see this,' she said drily. 'I've just been convincing him that bedrooms were out of bounds.'

'A novel idea for him,' he said darkly.

'Oh, it was all very light-hearted. He's no more of a threat than you are.'

She saw from the look on his face that he had not found the remark flattering. She had not intended it to be so.

'If you're capable of taking a warning, I wouldn't advise you to allow Jean-Paul any rein. Over the years I've heard quite a bit about his over-active libido. No——' he could see that she was about to protest, and raised an autocratic hand to silence her '—hear me out, will you? Jean-Paul is the *cadet*—the youngest, the baby of the family. He has been cosseted and adored by every female relative for the whole of his charmed life—and not only by relatives. He has the idea as far as any woman is concerned that what he wants, he gets.' He paused.

'You mean that he may have it in mind to nip into the nearest hotel with me at some point and extend the scope of the relationship?' Alex asked coolly.

He looked displeased. 'If you have to put it so crudely.'

'Why not? It's a pretty crude suggestion, isn't it? No point dressing it up in pretty words.' Green eyes glared into grey.

'I merely intended to point out that what you might consider natural friendliness could be misinterpreted by someone of a different background. I wouldn't want anyone to walk into a situation that proved embarrassing, that's all,' he said curtly. 'You are, after all——'

'Your responsibility,' she finished for him with an air of delicate boredom. 'Look, Marcus, don't treat me like a kid from infant school. I don't want to be looked after by anyone—least of all you—and as far as today is concerned I see no need for it. We're going to do a bit of sightseeing, that's all. I hardly think Jean-Paul has it in mind to grab me by the hair and drag me off to the nearest cave. Nor do I think he's the type to inflict himself on an unwilling partner.' This last was said with a challenging look that conveyed a clear memory of Marcus's behaviour the night before.

'What about a partner who may start off unwilling but change her mind with surprising rapidity?' he retorted with stinging sarcasm.

'I think that would be my business.'

'And as usual you have a closed mind to any suggestion for your welfare.'

'Not at all. You stressed that you wanted good relations with our hosts. I have accepted the offer of an outing with the brother of our hostess. How much more obliging and obedient and open to suggestion can I get? Jean-Paul is not an unknown lorry driver. He's not some stranger I've met in the deserted countryside. He's a perfectly charming and pleasant acquaintance. And now, if you don't mind, I must go. I'm keeping him waiting. Don't worry. I'm sure we'll have a lovely time.' She gave him an infuriating smile and saw the effect of it in the flash of silver in his eyes and the movement of a muscle in his jaw, then, with a flounce of the full skirt of her dress, she left him.

Jean-Paul came out of the dining-room as she reached the hall.

'Ah! *Chouette*!' he said, expressing approval of her dress. 'And sandals that are good for walking as well. Not just a pretty face, don't you say?'

'Does Christiane know we are going now?' Alex asked.

'Yes. I have spoken to her. We are quite official! So, *mademoiselle*, let's go.'

He was entertaining, charming, and utterly circumspect until mid-afternoon in Rouen, when he gave way to what he called an irresistible urge and kissed Alex unexpectedly while they were looking at the statue of Joan of Arc.

What do I feel? Alex asked herself. The answer was— nothing. It was a kiss like a million others, and, expert though Jean-Paul no doubt was in the art of love, he set alight not one tiny spark of the shameful, illicit fire that Marcus's touch had set blazing in her last night.

Jean-Paul was quick to sense her attitude.

'You are angry?' he asked as they began to walk back to the car again.

She took his hand and squeezed it. 'Not at all! How could I be when you're giving me such a lovely day?'

'Then it must be a case of no anger, but no rapture either,' he said. 'Don't deny it, *ma petite*. I am an expert when it comes to the temperature of a kiss.'

Alex gave a protesting laugh. 'It's a bit early to be talking of rapture. We've only just met.'

'That has nothing to do with the case. If the magic is there, time and circumstance have no meaning.' He looked down at her. 'Suppose I had been Marcus, just now...'

'Marcus!' Her voice was full of scorn. 'He can't bear me.'

He looked knowingly at her. 'When a lady protests so vehemently, then there is something in the air.'

'Nothing more than straightforward dislike. Our families have been beating the hell out of each other for three generations.'

'And what have families to do with what happens between a man and a woman?' Jean-Paul asked scathingly.

'Jean-Paul! Believe me! We fight like cat and dog all the time.'

'*Voilà*!' he said, as though she had proved the point indisputably. 'Love and hate are very close emotions. Love and indifference couldn't be further apart.' He looked accusingly at her. 'Don't tell me he has never kissed you. How could he resist?'

At the thought of the previous night, Alex blushed.

'I see that you know more than you are willing to say,' he teased. 'Come and have some of the tea you English love, and tell me about families and quarrels...' he ran a finger over the pink of her cheek '... and what causes this charming betrayal of the words you have so far refused to say.'

Alex gave way to the urge to talk to someone, and when she had finished recounting the sorry history of Marcus and Elaine Jean-Paul sat back, frowning.

'It doesn't sound at all like the Marcus I know and have known for several years,' he said.

'Then doesn't it prove how utterly sick he must have been to find that once again he had been deceived into something by a member of the Leeward family?'

He looked at her with sympathy. 'You have managed to place yourself at the centre of a Montague-Capulet situation, it seems, *ma belle* Alex.'

'No!' she said vehemently. 'Haven't I just been telling you how impossible it is for there to be anything other than dislike between Marcus and myself?'

He took her hand, planted a light kiss in its palm, and closed her fingers over the spot. 'Very well, *ma petite*,' he said soothingly. 'You are not the least bit in love, if that is what it pleases you to think. Now let's forget the unfortunate subject and enjoy ourselves again.'

It was late when they arrived back at the Château after dining at a riverside restaurant at Les Andelys, a setting made dramatic by a gathering storm piling clouds in the sky and whipping up waves on the water.

Albertine was the only one at the Château. Rémy and family had left for home during the course of the day, and the others had gone to a *son et lumière* some miles away.

Alex went over to check on the horses, though Albertine insisted that they had been fed and Mistral had had her night-time injection, and as she came back it started to pour down. There was a certain malicious satisfaction in the thought of Marcus getting soaked somewhere in the dark night. She excused herself and went up to bed, leaving Jean-Paul watching a late film on television.

Once she was in bed, the thoughts to which Jean-Paul had given life returned to the forefront of Alex's mind with full force. It wasn't true, it couldn't possibly be true, that there was anything between herself and Marcus other than a kind of basic physical response on her part. A response that reflected nothing but shame on her, and which was to be stamped out at all costs.

She applied reason to the situation. She had been too long without a serious boyfriend. That was it. One kiss from a passably attractive man, and her hormones ran riot, no matter who he was.

So why did the same set of hormones behave with such restraint when Jean-Paul kissed her? Answer that one, smart Alex, her mind taunted unpleasantly.

She turned over and buried her face in the pillow, plagued by a host of worrying thoughts while the rain beat a tattoo against the shutters until finally she fell asleep.

She was roused by the most violent crack of thunder she had ever heard. The storm must be right overhead. She sat up, seeing the brilliant flash of lightning through the chinks of the shutters. The thunder cracked again and there was the sizzling, searing hiss of electricity earthing itself frighteningly close.

The horses! They would be terrified.

Alex leapt out of bed and ran for the door, pulling on the silk kimono over her mouse-appliquéd pyjamas. The bedroom doors were open as she ran along the corridor. She had no idea what time it was or how long she had slept, but the rest of the party were not back yet. She went swiftly downstairs and ran through the rain round to the stables.

Mistral and Lasco, who normally slept lying down close to each other in a way that was quite individual to them, were standing huddled in a corner of the stall, whinnying restlessly, and when the lightning flashed again Alex saw the whites of their eyes as they rolled in fear.

'It's all right, little ones,' she told them. 'You're safe in here. It'll soon be over.' She dug out a couple of apples from the sack in the next stall and fed them to the two horses, then stood between them, a hand on each, talking softly and calmingly to them. She could feel their quickened breathing, and worried that it would aggravate Mistral's cough. She would stay with them until the worst of the storm had passed over, she decided.

After a while, when the thunder had lost the worst of its violence, Lasco settled down on the straw and Mistral, after a bit of restless shuffling, followed suit. But as the little horse made herself comfortable a brief fit of dry coughing plagued her. Alex drew over a blanket and sat down beside her, carrying on with the soothing murmur of talk and the gentle movement of her hand over the rough white coat. Gradually the lightning began to flash less fiercely. It was dark and warm in the stable. Alex's head drooped and rested against Mistral's flank. Just a little longer she would wait. Just a few minutes more until she was sure that Mistral was not going to cough again... It was really very comfortable sitting like this, with her head rising and falling gently as the little horse's breathing grew calm. The storm rumbled and rolled away into the distance, and the stable was full of drowsy peace.

Alex stirred at a sound which could have been her name, then lapsed into sleep again. It was something like the soft, caressing touch of lips on her forehead that really began to wake her. She put up a hand and felt a face close to hers, wriggled sleepily and said in a half-laughing murmur without opening her eyes, 'Jean-Paul! You're incorrigible!'

'Wake up, and get up!' a voice that was definitely not Jean-Paul's said harshly.

Alex's eyes flew open, and she saw Marcus standing over her, a paraffin lamp in his hand. His hair was glistening wet, as were the shoulders of his Barbour jacket. The familiar expression of total displeasure was on his face.

'You!' Her heart gave a sickening jolt as she realised that it was his face she had touched just now. 'You're dripping on me!' she said, hiding her confusion in accusation as she scrambled to her feet. 'You're wet through.'

'And definitely not lover-boy,' he said sarcastically.

Alex blushed at his reference to the manner of her waking, and her hand went involuntarily to her lips. 'I thought——' she began, then stopped suddenly. If she said somebody she had taken for Jean-Paul had kissed her, then that implied, since Marcus was the only person there, that she imagined he had done so...and it had been such a gentle, tender dream kiss, the kind he would never in a million years give her.

'You thought what?' he said curtly.

'Nothing. I was dreaming.'

'Walked out here in your sleep, did you?'

'Of course I didn't.' Alex was beginning to regain her senses. 'The storm woke me and I thought the horses might be frightened. They were very disturbed so I stood and talked to them for a bit, then Mistral coughed, so I got her settled down and stayed on for a while. I must have fallen asleep. Is it very late?'

'Two o'clock.' He looked round suspiciously. 'I presume you're alone?'

'Oh, don't be so ridiculous!' she snapped, switching to the attack. 'And talking of the ridiculous, why on earth did you sit out in the pouring rain all this time?'

'The *son et lumière* stopped when the extra sound effects got too much. But our crazy hosts insisted on going to a Vietnamese restaurant afterwards where we steamed the place out. We shall probably all develop pneumonia.'

'Jean-Paul and I were back here at ten-thirty,' she said virtuously. 'Have you seen him? He was going to watch a film that went on until the small hours.'

'Yes, I have seen him, unfortunately,' Marcus said with barely suppressed fury.

'What do you mean, "unfortunately"?'

He looked balefully at her. 'I suppose the fool will be dying to tell you about it if I don't. When I went upstairs, your bedroom door was wide open and you were nowhere to be seen. The bathrooms were empty, and I knew you weren't downstairs. So I jumped to the obvious conclusion.'

'Only obvious to someone with a mind like yours. And did what?' Alex asked coldly.

'I did what any responsible person would have done. I barged into Jean-Paul's room ready to knock him into the middle of next week——'

'What an appallingly silly thing to do!' she exclaimed, exasperated.

'That was more or less Jean-Paul's verdict, only he was a bit less inhibited in his expression of it.'

'You're lucky he didn't go for you,' she said, wishing Jean-Paul had done just that.

He sneered. 'He wouldn't dare. Mauling women's about his limit.'

'He, at least, behaved impeccably today.'

'I've only your word for that.' They glared at each other until Alex turned angrily away.

'I'm going back. This is a pointless conversation. I don't know why you came over.'

He followed her to the door. 'Look out, and you'll soon know.' He flung the door wide, and where before there had been a moat and a broad walk off which the stable yard opened Alex now saw that there appeared to be just an alarmingly extended moat.

She gasped involuntarily. 'What on earth's happened?'

'Tim's bright idea of channelling a stream into the moat to keep it fresh has gone wrong. The culvert can't take the water away as fast as it comes flooding in.' He looked down at her feet, on which she was wearing a pair of flimsy mules. 'Suitably shod, aren't you?'

He made a move towards her and Alex recoiled nervously. 'Don't touch me!'

He looked scathingly at her. 'What do you think I have in mind? Before your imagination runs riot, let me tell you my only intention is to carry you back to the house. The power's gone as well. With no light from the windows you'd be likely to end up in the damned moat yourself.'

'I can take these off and paddle,' Alex said hurriedly.

'Don't be ridiculous.' Before she could protest further, he hoisted her up into his arms. For a moment he paused, looking down at her in the fitful moonlight as though he had forgotten what he was supposed to be doing, and then asked, his voice a degree or two softer, 'Where did you get this silky thing?'

'Christiane lent it to me.' She felt stiff and awkward, fiendishly embarrassed to be held by him. And her heart was pounding so loud that it seemed impossible for him not to hear it.

'It's a deal better than those pyjamas with the mouse on that you seem so fond of.' He hitched her up and said irritably, 'Try not to imitate a sack of potatoes. Put your arm round my neck and hang on, can't you?'

Alex did as she was told, glad of the darkness as he stepped out into the night. She tried to hold her head stiffly away from him, but he nudged it back against his shoulder with his hard chin and snarled, 'Give me a chance to see where I'm going, can't you?'

Neither of them spoke until he put her down at the top of the steps into the Château.

'Good job you're not overweight,' he said prosaically, hooking off his wellingtons against the edge of the top step.

They went into the hall where someone had left a small lamp burning on a low wick. Beside it there were two lighted candles.

'Do you need a drink to warm you?' Marcus asked.

She still felt far too conscious of the feel of his warmth, of the pulse in his neck as her face rested against it in that unexpected intimacy.

'No, thanks,' she said, avoiding his eyes. 'I'll go straight up.'

'Take one of the candles. It should give enough light for you to see your way upstairs.'

'Yes, thanks. Goodnight.' She felt as awkward and tongue-tied as a teenager.

'Goodnight,' he said indifferently. But after a couple of seconds he called, almost fiercely, 'A pretty memorable time he gave you, did he?'

She stopped and looked down at him, at the warm gold of his hair, drying now, and at the grey eyes staring angrily up at her.

She felt a rush of tears to her eyes, and had an overwhelming urge to cry out that nothing Jean-Paul could do could affect her as much as the precious few seconds while he, Marcus, had carried her back from the stables and she'd felt the roughness of his end-of-the-day skin and been aware of the strong beat of his heart and the pine-fresh smell of the soap he had used. The strength of her feelings frightened her. How would he react if she gave him a truthful answer like that? She tore her eyes away from his and said lamely, 'It was just a day out...' then hurried up the dark staircase.

He had been concerned about light. There was enough light for her to see where she was going in this house, but the future—that was a different matter. The future suddenly seemed more dark and cloudy and complex than it had ever been.

It was no use fooling herself any longer. She was either going mad or she was falling in love with the man who should be the object of her hatred. Perhaps she was doing both. Why him? Why the *hell* him? The question shrieked in her tortured mind. She loved her sister and her father, didn't she? She hated what Marcus Wakeford had done to them. There was no need to question that. But here she was, in spite of it all, apparently unable to stop this crazy course she was on. She sat on her bed in the moonlight, feeling more frightened than she had ever been in her life and clinging to the edge of the mattress as though her grip on that were the only thing that could stop her falling off the world.

CHAPTER SEVEN

ALEX spent most of the night trying to face up to her state of mind and heart. Admitting that there was something about Marcus that transcended all the ill feeling between them and called forth an unwanted and frightening response from her was one thing. Reconciling herself to the guilt she felt on her sister's and father's behalf because of it was in quite a different category. Full daylight found her still awake and wretched, and her mirror showed her a pale, worried face with dark shadows under her eyes. She didn't want to face any of the others at breakfast, and went straight over to the stables, only to be tracked down there by Marcus.

Her heart gave the usual dizzy lurch at the sight of him but she was able to disguise it by pretending not to know he was there in the doorway watching her.

'Why no breakfast?' he asked, forcing her to look up and acknowledge his presence.

'I didn't feel like it.'

He took down the saddles and passed Mistral's over to her. 'That's all right, then. We can get off to the vet's straight away. Unless,' he added drily, 'you don't feel like riding either.'

'That's not an option. It's my job. But I'm glad to think you consider Mistral fit to be ridden again,' she said quietly, busying herself with the saddle.

Half an hour later the vet confirmed that the little horse was indeed much better, and said that he was sure that they would have no trouble at the port if they decided to be on their way in the morning.

'That's good,' Marcus said with evident relief. He looked at Alex. 'And I know you'll be glad to be on your way again.'

'Very glad,' Alex echoed, torn between relief at the prospect of the end of the ordeal and a cruel stab of pain at the thought of the inevitable parting from the man who had had such a profound effect on her emotions.

For the rest of today, with a bit of luck she could keep out of his way, then tomorrow they would be crossing the Channel with only a few more miles on English soil to cover.

She was thunderstruck when Marcus said suddenly as they were riding back, 'Once we've made calls home to let people know when to expect us, we'll go off for the rest of the day.'

'Whatever for?' Alex asked, stunned into rudeness by the unexpectedness of the suggestion.

He gave her a withering look. 'For a very good reason. I run a workforce of over a hundred in one place and another, and deal with God knows how many times as many clients. Everything operates smoothly, pleasantly, efficiently. I'm blowed if I'm going to arrive home feeling that a pint-sized girl can never fail to get under my skin and ruffle my temper. I'll make you pass a few civilised hours with me, I'm damned if I won't. And I'm suggesting a day out—not a session in a torture chamber, for God's sake!'

'But——' Alex began.

'But nothing. We're going to see if we can manage to be polite to each other for an hour or two. So kindly hold your tongue and put up with it.'

'Not a very promising beginning,' she said drily.

He glared at her and trotted ahead on Lasco. Mistral broke into a trot too, and Alex wondered wretchedly how on earth she was going to survive this latest ordeal.

There was no reprieve back at the Château where Tim recommended a little restaurant in a neighbouring village, and told them of a walk they could do after lunch if they felt so inclined. He was both literally and metaphorically up to his neck in the moat, and as soon as she knew it was to be their last night Christiane promised them a party. Full of apprehension for both the party and the unwanted outing, Alex eventually got into the Range Rover beside Marcus.

The pleasantness of the surroundings in the quaint little restaurant helped, and the food certainly lived up to Tim's recommendation. They ate a delicious *pâté de campagne maison* followed by pheasant cooked *à la normande* on a bed of apples, cream and Calvados, and accompanied by a delicious mixed salad with walnuts. But the atmosphere between the two eaters fell far short of the standard of the food. Marcus kept up a flow of polished conversation as though he were entertaining a business guest, but all Alex could think of was the hopelessness of two such alienated people attempting to achieve anything like a sociable atmosphere. And, worse than that, she felt that the ghosts of her sister and her father were invisible spectators, and her eyes slid away from Marcus's when he, with a kind of fierce determination, would have held her gaze.

She hoped and prayed that he would decide against Tim's suggested walk, but that was apparently another challenge that had to be faced. Seeming preoccupied now, but still determined, Marcus led the way through countryside washed clean and fresh after last night's storm. The hot morning sunshine had dried up the rain as though it had never been. The path took them up a hill and out beyond the trees to a rocky high point, from which the lush green rural landscape could be seen in all directions.

There was a grassy hollow a few feet down the opposite side of the slope, and they made for it, sitting down to look their fill in silence, Alex thinking thankfully that this farce of a day must soon be over.

At last Marcus spoke. 'Since we'll be on our way tomorrow and you'll be meeting Becky at the end of the day, there's something I should tell you.'

Alex looked at him. 'Yes?'

'I have the impression that you think her a spoiled brat.' The words sounded harsh though they were said in a neutral, almost matter-of-fact way.

'I haven't said any such thing,' Alex demurred.

'Not in so many words.' He gave her an ironical look. 'But, with a face as transparent as yours, you don't often need to verbalise what you're feeling.'

'Then I wish you wouldn't do it for me. Unexpressed feelings are private.' She wondered how much her face had given away of her feelings for him. To know that he was aware of how she was beginning to feel about him would be the ultimate humiliation.

To her relief he said, 'It's Becky's feelings that concern me most right now, with the prospect of you actually meeting her tomorrow. On our first night at the Château you pretended to need confirmation of the child's existence—though how that can be when you have obviously discussed me at some length with your precious sister I fail to see.'

'Elaine *is* my precious sister!' Alex said in hot defence, responding quickly to the sarcasm in his tone. 'Just as Becky is your precious Becky.'

He looked searchingly at her. 'But the question I ask myself is, are you cast in the same mould as your sister?'

'How can I not be? We have the same parents, the same family name, the same upbringing.'

'And feelings? Do you share your sister's feelings?'

Oh, yes, Alex thought bitterly. I share her feelings in every respect, even to the extent of beginning to love the same man, but I'm crazier than she, because I have her word for it that there's no future for a Leeward and a Wakeford.

'Inevitably, on some subjects. Not on all,' she said with difficulty.

'All right. Let's take the subject of physical disability. Becky is quite badly handicapped. Would you prefer not to be confronted with that?'

The question struck her as being so outrageous that she responded indignantly, 'How can you ask something like that? I spend most of my working life with people who have one disability or another. Would I choose and stay in that kind of work if I couldn't cope with it?'

'I had to ask,' he said unrepentantly. 'When the subject of Becky first came up, we didn't get round to that particular aspect. We got...side-tracked, if you remember.'

Did she remember? Would she ever forget that night in the barn...the way he had silenced her when she'd implied that compensating a child who had lost both parents with lavish gifts might not be the answer? She was trying desperately hard to forget how she had reacted to that kiss. One kiss—it was no big deal. She ought to be able to forget it. She *must*.

'Becky has been handicapped from birth,' he was going on. 'At the moment, she couldn't walk without the calipers she wears on both legs.' His voice softened as he went on almost huskily, 'The handicap is purely physical. In no way does it affect her spirit. When it comes to sheer guts, she's larger and more sound than life. I imagine that slightly changes the mental picture of her that you have.'

'I think you must derive real pleasure from insulting me,' Alex said in a choked voice, looking down at her clenched hands.

'I have no thought of insulting anyone. But there is nothing I wouldn't do to defend and protect Becky from any more hurt. Life has flung enough at her already.' He looked out over the countryside, and a smile played round the corner of his mouth. 'She wouldn't like to hear me say that—and the simple truth is that I quite honestly don't think of her as being handicapped most of the time. When you meet her you'll understand why. She's not an object of pity. She's a plucky little girl—a born fighter. That's the image of her that stays in the mind—not what she has to fight against.'

'What happened to her parents?' Alex pretended close interest in a clump of grass on the side of her away from him. She was doing her own bit of fighting at the moment. The way he talked about his charge and the picture he painted of the little girl who was so different from the child she had imagined almost had her in tears.

'They got caught up in one of those inexplicable pile-ups in fog on the motorway. Killed instantly.'

Alex swallowed with difficulty. 'And Becky survived?'

'She wasn't involved. She was in hospital at the time, recovering from one of the many operations she's had in her short life. Jake and Tricia had been there with her, of course, but there were things they needed from home, and once she was over the worst they drove back to Sussex to collect them. They were on the way back to London when it happened. Becky was used to hospitals, but, as you can imagine, this operation has left her with different associations from the rest. She's due to go in again in about six months from now. You can picture the danger this time. She's going to be remembering that hospital is linked with the loss of people she loves. That's why, when she developed this passion for a Camargue horse, I decided she should have one. Maybe if she can fix her mind on getting back to her beloved horse she won't be dragged down by other thoughts.'

When Alex didn't answer, he turned to look at her and saw the tears brimming over from her eyes.

'Don't cry,' he said, almost gently. 'Becky doesn't cry for herself. She'd hate anyone else to cry for her.'

Alex gave a huge, gulping sob. 'For God's sake, don't be nice to me!' she choked, the crying beginning in earnest.

'Alex!' Forgetting who she was for a moment, it seemed, he put an arm round her and held her against the smooth cotton of his shirt, stroking her hair and letting her cry her fill. She felt more confused than she had ever been in her life. Why was she crying? Partly for Becky, but also for the mess in which she found herself. Everything Marcus told her about himself chipped away at the picture she had previously had of him. It had been so easy to hate him before she knew him, but every minute of every day made it more difficult to hold on to what she ought to be feeling about him. She felt as though she had been disloyal to him now, as well as to her family.

In desperation she turned and clutched him like a frightened child, burying her face more deeply against his neck. At first she thought his arms had tightened round her, but then she realised that he was firmly if gently holding her away from him.

'Let's not go over the top,' he said almost humorously, obviously totally unaware of the turmoil of emotion ravaging her.

Alex's confused feelings veered again and erupted in fury. Her face red, her eyes streaming, she said in irrational contradiction of everything she had just been thinking about him, 'Of course, I should have remembered. The Wakefords don't have feelings. Only a cold-blooded capacity for decision-making.'

His expression changed. 'Is that your considered opinion?' he said dangerously. 'Yet another of your clanging mistakes. Let's see if I can convince you otherwise.' There was only time for a brief, frightening glimpse of blazing eyes, then Alex was pushed back on the turf and his weight was pressing the breath out of her. His mouth smothered her cry of alarm in a kiss that

punished as roughly as any blow and seemed to go on
forever until she thought she would suffocate. At last,
breathing harshly, he released her and sat up, looking
contemptuously down at her.

'Was that good enough for you?' he asked scathingly.

'That wasn't feeling!' she flung at him as she
scrambled away in undignified, clumsy haste. 'That was
brute strength. And I mean brute.'

'Give you what you ask for, and you don't want it.
You're as changeable and unpredictable as your sister.'
He stood up. 'But at least it appears to have put an end
to the waterworks. So perhaps we can do something
useful and finish this damned walk.'

He waited until she had scrambled to her feet, then
set off down the hill. Alex followed, calling after him
when she had the breath to do so, her voice tight with
fury, 'I would like to go straight back, please.'

'Don't worry!' he shouted angrily over his shoulder.
'I've had enough, too.'

What hurt more than the bruised lips, the hurt pride,
she thought in her room at the Château as she did her
packing, was the knowledge that even that humiliating
memory was something she apparently wanted to hang
on to.

She had caught herself fingering the little folder of
matches she had slipped into her bag in the restaurant
where they'd eaten their awkward lunch. It was a pub-
licity gimmick with a line drawing of the picturesque
little stone building.

Contemptuous of herself, she put it away with the red
cocarde from the horns of the bull—the 'spoils for the
lady'. Reminders, both of them, not only of a shining
fair head and grey eyes that could go from silver-warm
to flint-cold, but of her own feeble loyalty and incipient
treachery. Maybe as reminders of the latter they were
worth keeping.

She sighed heavily, and covered the pathetic little souvenirs with more prosaic items. If only she had never met Liz, back in the Camargue. Any amount of difficulty in getting home would have been preferable to finding herself in the same position as her sister—easily bewitched by an impossible man. Only how much more foolish was she than Elaine. All along she had known from Elaine's sad example that nothing good could come of this association between a Leeward and a Wakeford. And still she had allowed herself to be burned by the fire she should never have played with.

She sighed again. No matter. It was almost over. Tomorrow was for England, home and sanity. And the chance to find out if there was truth in the old saying 'out of sight, out of mind'.

Christiane had refused all offers of help with the party food, saying that as one of the guests of honour Alex should come down to find everything a huge surprise. The sitting-room and dining-room were out of bounds, she was told, and her only option once she had seen to the feeding and comfort of the horses was to take as long as possible over the process of getting ready.

It was, therefore, a *soignée* and elegant Alex who emerged from her room at seven-thirty, determined to hide her shattered spirit behind an impeccable appearance. She was wearing her other big summer purchase, a slim-fitting black sheath that left her shoulders bare, its simple square neck evolving into straps that crossed the smooth sun-kissed skin of her back to fasten with the dress's only ornament, two chased gold buttons. Against the dark simplicity of the dress her hair shone like burnished copper. Apart from her gold chain, she had limited her jewellery to Mexican earrings in the form of clusters of tiny gold bells. The delicate sound they made seemed other-worldly. She thought fiercely that any other world would be preferable to her own at the moment.

Tim hurried over as she entered the sitting-room, threading his way through the dozen or more guests assembled, and taking her round to meet everyone.

'You would never think, to look at this vision of beauty, that she is capable of working as hard as any man in a stable, would you?' he jokingly asked the last couple to be introduced. Jean-Paul overheard.

'Certainly not. Link her with unicorns, not horses, and that would be far more credible. *Tu es belle ce soir, princesse,*' he said softly in Alex's ear, expertly drawing her aside.

'Putting on the old Gallic charm tonight, are you, Jean-Paul?' Marcus said, joining them in time to hear the compliment. The look in his eyes was at odds with his pleasant tone of voice. He turned to Alex. 'Good evening, Alex. Sophistication for you, I see.'

'Is that the Englishman's idea of a flattering remark?' Jean-Paul mocked, one hand curving round Alex's arm in a proprietorial way. 'No wonder you English girls come to the Continent with an air of starvation about you.'

'Starvation? I thought it was a look of distaste for all the verbal froth they hear,' Marcus said coolly. 'They haven't had a diet of it from the cradle, remember.'

Jean-Paul laughed good-humouredly, but there was a touch of malice in his answer. 'Since there is such understanding between you fellow-English, I shall try out some of my pretty words on Alex during dinner, and see what she makes of them. Oh—do I see my sister trying to catch your attention, Marcus?'

When Marcus turned to look in the direction Jean-Paul was pointing, the Frenchman, with a finger to his lips, whisked Alex away through the door towards the dining-room.

Alex had been feeling like someone caught on a battlefield where cross-fire was about to break out. She could sense that Marcus was ready for a fight with anyone. He had belligerence emanating from every pore and she was glad to be away from him, but she had little patience for Jean-Paul's badinage.

'I don't remember promising to be your table companion at dinner,' she told him.

'No table—it's a buffet. But you would have agreed to partner me if I had asked, wouldn't you?' he said unrepentantly. 'How could you resist me?'

'Very easily. But I can't resist Albertine's lovely food, so I'll agree to have you as an incidental accompaniment.'

'*Belle et cruelle*!' he said. 'An intriguing combination and one it would be amusing to study. But first let's eat. Do not, by the way, look in Marcus's direction while doing so. His expression would be likely to give you indigestion.'

Several times as the evening progressed Alex caught Marcus's dangerous silver gaze resting on her, but he didn't seek another exchange with Jean-Paul. Nor did he make any attempt to come near her for a long time. She told herself she was glad of it, but she was never unaware of his exact position in the room, never without the slight unease of wondering what he was thinking.

Tim had strung lights between the trees to the west of the Château and run an extension across the moat so that he could play music for dancing. Alex was in great demand, and Jean-Paul made sure that she spent much of the time pressed against his eager young frame.

'Do you have to do that?' Alex asked as he gave her a bit of excessively Gallic attention when they danced close to Marcus and his partner.

'Why not? I may be on to a loser with you, *ma belle*, but I regard it as my mission in life to stir up as many Englishmen as possible.' He caught and ignored a particularly malevolent look from Marcus. 'Unless I am mistaken, though, our dear Marcus has taken as much stirring as he can put up with for one evening. He is heading towards us with an air of great determination. Prepare yourself for action, *ma chère* Alex.' He swung her round with a flourish, laughing down into her face.

Marcus tapped him on the shoulder. 'On your way, Jean-Paul. This is my dance.' He was smiling as he spoke for the benefit of the surrounding couples, but the smile was strongly contradicted by the dangerous light in his eyes.

Jean-Paul took a further couple of steps. 'And what if I don't agree?'

Marcus's smile took on the character of a baring of teeth and his voice would have sliced through metal. 'I shall chuck you in the moat. Don't doubt it for a second.'

Jean-Paul prudently relinquished his hold on Alex. 'Then, since I have no desire for the two of us to look ridiculous, and since you put it so nicely, Marcus...' he said, stepping aside with a knowing look at Alex and a mocking bow in Marcus's direction.

'Throwing your weight around again, Marcus?' Alex queried tensely as he took her none too gently into his arms.

'No more than he deserves, the posturing, self-appreciating twit!' he said viciously. His hand on the bare skin of her back forced her nearer to him, and his voice was harsh in her ear. 'Since you've been closer to your French admirer than a sticking plaster for the past two dances, perhaps you could stop giving the impression that we're two repelling magnetic poles.'

'That's just what we are, I thought,' Alex said, but her body refused to obey her mind and imperceptibly she allowed herself to soften against him. Allowed? Who was she fooling? She couldn't stop herself—for she was no longer a free agent when she was close to Marcus. She was powerless to remain stiffly hostile under his touch.

Why should it be? she asked herself desperately as they moved slowly in time to the music. Was it the attraction of the forbidden? Was the impossible always more appealing than the readily available? She knew how useless it was to allow any reaction to Marcus to take her over, but she seemed unable to help it. Neither loyalty to her sister and father nor sensible concern for her own welfare seemed to work against the bewildering assault on her senses when he touched her. The sooner they were on their way tomorrow the better. But even while she strove to cling to this thought her body was aware in every fibre of how perfectly it fitted against his, and how much it would like this dance to go on forever.

The record ended and another began. Alex made an unsuccessful attempt to free herself from the arms that held her so determinedly.

'You've won your point against Jean-Paul. Why insist on going on dancing with me?' she said helplessly.

'To convince everyone that all's well. It's a great party and we're having a wonderful time,' he said, his voice sarcastic. He pressed her still closer against him, and even with the evidence of his hostility in her ear the contact was bittersweet to her, not repugnant as it should have been. One record gave way to another, and without speaking the two of them danced on. As the third record came to an end, Alex felt his grip release her and looked up at him as though in a daze.

'That should have done the trick,' he said, looking dispassionately down at her. 'Thank you for the pleasure, Miss Leeward. I think we can rejoin the rest of the party now.'

He didn't come near her again until the guests were leaving and Jean-Paul, Tim, Christiane and the two of them stood waving goodnight, watching the car lights illumine the trees one by one, and then give way to darkness. They turned indoors to do a perfunctory tidy-up before going to bed, leaving the serious washing-up

until morning, 'After you've gone,' Christiane told Alex
regretfully, adding as the two of them collected glasses
from the sitting-room, 'It's been lovely to have you here.
I hope—no, I feel sure—that Marcus will be bringing
you back to see us again before long.'

'No, he won't, really,' Alex said forlornly. 'This truly
was just a business arrangement. As private individuals,
we're poles apart.'

Christiane put her head on one side, considering Alex
with amusement. 'I saw you dancing together. Body
language speaks more than words.'

Alex blushed. 'But it can lie. I was half asleep, that's
all.'

'*Ma chère* Alex,' Christiane said with tolerant
amusement, 'I know an English expression that answers
your excuse perfectly. "Tell it to the Marines"! However,
we shall see.'

Side by side, not speaking, thinking their individual
thoughts, Alex and Marcus stood leaning on the rail of
the ferry, watching the French port shrink and fade into
the distance as the stretch of sea on which the ferry left
its wake increased. In Dieppe the vet had pronounced
both horses fit, and the long journey with them was
almost over.

'Have you decided what you're going to do?' Marcus
asked abruptly. 'As far as work is concerned, I mean.'

'More or less. I want to stay in hospital work, and I
shall try to get another post in the National Health
Service.'

'You surprise me.'

'Why? The NHS trained me, after all.'

He looked impassively at her. 'I thought you might
come down in favour of self-interest and go for the
money in private medicine.'

'Well, you were wrong,' she said tiredly, not rising to
the offence implicit in his words.

They watched the gulls over the wake in silence for a moment or two.

'Becky must be feeling excited right now,' Alex said eventually, beginning to find the silence heavy.

'She made me work out exactly how long it would take us from Newhaven to the house. She also made it clear that we're expected to arrive on horseback, not towing. Can I ask you to go along with that?'

Alex glanced at him. 'You're the boss.'

'You've been very helpful,' he said stiffly. 'I'm sorry it's turned out to be such a long trip back.'

She shrugged. 'That was nobody's fault.'

He straightened up. 'We're nearing the end now, anyway. Another three and a half hours to the harbour, then a drive that will seem nothing after the distance we've covered. I'm going to get some coffee. Coming?'

Alex's eyes were still on the fading coast of France. 'Not just yet. I'll come down in a while.'

He left her without any further attempt to persuade her to accompany him. In all probability he was as relieved to leave her as she was to have him go. It was so hard to be near him. But they were on a British boat, heading for British shores. Once they were back in Sussex where the quarrel of the Wakefords and Leewards had its roots, then the turmoil of confusing emotions in her would be seen for what it was—the product of a foreign land and of unwanted proximity...a glancing blow from fate.

They had crossed on the one forty-five boat—the first possible after the formalities of the port. It was early evening when they docked in Newhaven, and the sun was low in the sky by the time they had driven across the county towards the Cuckmere Valley where Chessetts, Marcus's house, nestled in a fold of the Downs.

Marcus put on his *gardian's* hat as they prepared for the triumphal ride over the last stage to Chessetts.

'Another promise I had to make,' he said ruefully. 'It looks a little out of place here, don't you think?'

Alex, struggling with her private memory of the first time she had seen him, a strangely unreal, almost mythical figure in his white clothes, on his white horse, with the black *gardian's* hat in stunning contrast with the bright gold of his hair, made no reply.

The house was long and low, with a rambling old wistaria climbing over its door and across the white stucco between the ground- and first-floor windows.

They had no sooner turned into the curving drive than a small figure appeared in the doorway and came hurrying towards them. The calipers she had on both thin legs seemed no impediment. The child almost flew over the ground until she stood fearlessly in the path of the two horses. She was slight and delicate-looking with dark, curling hair tied back in a single bunch and wide, excited eyes.

As the horses stopped, she went straight to Mistral and reached for the horse's bridle. The white horse lowered her head inquisitively to investigate the vivid little face turned up in delight, blew softly into the child's neck, and gave a low whinny. Her hand fingering the long white mane, her face pressed against the warm muzzle, the little girl uttered a soft, expressive, 'O-o-o-h!'

Marcus and Alex dismounted, and Marcus said, his tone amused, 'Well, hello, Becky! No need to ask what your priorities are!'

'O-o-o-h, Uncle Marcus!' she said, her voice muffled against his midriff. 'She's perfect!' She reached out to Lasco. 'And you are too!'

Marcus looked down at her, grinning broadly, and it seemed to Alex she was seeing a different man, uncomplicated and gentle now. 'No doubt that they've found favour with you, young lady.'

For the first time Becky seemed to become aware of Alex and gave her a shy smile.

'This is Alex, who has looked after Mistral all the way home. She'll be able to tell you all about her vices and virtues,' Marcus said.

'Hello, Becky.' Alex smiled reassuringly. 'Don't worry—she hasn't got any bad points as long as you remember to go easy on the legs and reins.'

'That's lucky. My wimpy legs will suit her very well, then,' Becky said quite unselfconsciously. 'May I ride her round to the stables, Uncle Marcus? Please! Anna and I have got both stalls ready with nuts and hay and water and everything.'

'Where is Anna?' Marcus said, looking towards the house. 'I thought she would have been part of the reception committee.'

'She's had to go away,' Becky said carelessly. 'There's a letter telling you about it. *Please* may I ride Mistral?'

'Just a minute. Who's here with you, then, if Anna isn't?'

'Mrs Ellerton's been here all day. It's all right, really, Uncle Marcus. Please may I——'

He swung her up into the saddle. 'Just round to the stable, then. And with Alex leading you, because this saddle isn't right for you.' His eyes were worried when he turned to Alex. 'Do you mind? I must find out what's going on. Anna's the king-pin around here.'

Alex took a firm hold of Mistral, with Lasco's bridle in her other hand. 'We'll be fine. When you're ready, Becky.'

'On second thoughts, put the horses in the paddock for the time being,' he called after them. 'I've a feeling that there won't be time to exercise them properly tonight.'

When she and Becky got back to the house, Alex could tell at once that Marcus was very worried, but he frowned and quietly signalled no questions, and talked to Becky while she had her bedtime drink. Becky wanted Alex to come upstairs and see her bedroom, so it was half an hour or so before he was able to tell her of the crisis that was on his hands.

'Anna's sister has had a heart attack, and there's no one else but Anna to sort things out for her and fix home care etcetera. She doesn't see herself being back for a week. I've phoned the agency we got Anna from—fortunately I had an emergency number—but it doesn't look very promising. All their regular people are in jobs, and two of the emergency nurses are down with flu. Damned tiresome.' He ran a distracted hand through his hair then looked at Alex. 'But you must be wanting to be off. There's a good meal waiting, it seems. They're ringing back from the agency, so we might as well eat.'

The agency call came halfway through the meal. Marcus came back looking grim.

'No go, I'm afraid. The only offer they could make for the next week was someone from Tuesday to Thursday. That's not much good. I simply have to be able to get back to work on Monday and have the whole week free. I've got two big audits to set up.'

'What about the lady who stood in today?'

'Mrs Ellerton? She works for other people too. Today's emergency was fine since it's Saturday, but she can't scrap her other commitments for a whole week.'

He helped himself to raspberries and ate in silence for a moment or two while Alex was preoccupied with her own thoughts. She was about to speak when he said, 'I can think of one or two local people who might take on the job for a week. When we get to the coffee stage, I'll take mine into the study if you don't mind and do a bit of ringing round.'

While she sipped her coffee, Alex could hear him making one call after another, and by the sound of it not meeting with any success.

'I've never come across so many busy people,' he said bitterly as he came back into the sitting-room. 'They've all got holidays booked or visitors coming or engagements solid throughout the week.' He looked at her. 'Look, don't let this hold you up. It's not your problem. I'll run you to the station when you're ready.'

She poured him more coffee, then took her courage in both hands. 'I can think of someone who isn't busy.' Even as she spoke her mind was saying to her, You're being an utter fool. Don't do it. But her lips paid no more heed to her mind than her body had done the night before when she was dancing with Marcus.

He looked enquiringly at her.

'Me,' she said simply, her heart pounding.

He stared at her, then said dismissively, 'You mean well, but I don't think either of us would relish the idea, would we? I think the past few days have been problematic enough without prolonging the situation.'

Having keyed herself up to make the suggestion, Alex was crushed by his attitude.

'I wasn't exactly contemplating a treat,' she said shortly. 'I was merely making an offer to meet the circumstances.'

'I realise that.' He frowned in concentration. 'There are still friends who might be willing to have Becky on their premises, though they couldn't live in here. Too much livestock of their own to take care of.'

'Are you remembering *your* recently purchased livestock? Farming Becky out would mean separating her from Mistral and Lasco. So soon after their arrival, wouldn't that be a refined form of torture?'

He looked hard at her. 'Be any more persuasive and you'll convince me that you'd actually like to stay on.'

'You can forget that idea,' Alex said fervently. 'My training encourages me to respond to an emergency, that's all.'

He stood there, lost in thought for a moment more. 'I'll try the Harcourts,' he said at last, and left the room. Alex wished she had never made the offer. Right now she felt just as strongly as he did that she had had enough and was a fool to contemplate more.

He came back almost instantly, obviously without having phoned anyone, his hair ruffled.

'You're right about the horses. Look—do you really think you could bear to stay on? I hate to ask you, knowing how you feel about things.'

'You didn't ask. I offered. And yes, I could bear it,' she said quietly, adding, because his attitude had been hurtful, 'In any case, you're not going to be around, are you? That should simplify matters.'

'Flattering, as always,' he murmured. She ignored him, suddenly dog-tired.

'And now, if you don't mind, I'd like to get rid of these dishes and then go to bed. Perhaps you'll show me where I can sleep.'

'Before I do that I'd better go and pick up the Range Rover or you won't have your mouse pyjamas. You needn't bother with the dishes. We can do them tomorrow, if you're tired.'

'Washing up doesn't bother me. I just don't feel like hanging around making conversation,' she told him bluntly.

His face darkened but his voice was restrained. 'Very well. I shan't be long.'

Alex carried out the coffee things to the kitchen. What on earth had she done? Another week of wishing she were miles away, and having it made obvious that her feelings were returned with interest by Marcus Wakeford.

What had got into her to persuade her to make that crazy offer? She clattered the dishes, knowing full well the answer to the question. And there was nothing noble about it, in spite of her high-flown words about training and responding to emergencies. Until she got Marcus's reluctant, lukewarm, last-ditch response to her suggestion, she had been motivated by something much less worthy than the desire to be helpful. There had been a mad wish—and how she regretted it now—for the experience of the past days to go on, for their ways not to separate.

Well, she had been a fool, and now she was going to have to pay for it. It was to be hoped that she could meet the cost.

CHAPTER EIGHT

APPREHENSIVE about the week ahead, Alex was awake early next morning. The house was still and silent, and, after lying drowsily watching the sheep on the lush green hillside she could see from her window for a while, she decided to go downstairs and familiarise herself with the kitchen arrangements before the actual need to do anything in there arose.

She found that Anna had left a list of reminders about Becky's various special items of equipment for school, and a helpful suggestion list for meals, indicating what food was available in the freezer and what would need to be shopped for. Obviously Anna was an extremely efficient woman who could think straight even when in the middle of a heart-attack situation. The kitchen was orderly, the cupboards fresh and tidy. Everything pointed to the fact that the standard of care provided by Anna was something to live up to.

When she had laid the table for breakfast it was almost eight o'clock. Alex made tea and carried the tray upstairs. On the landing she poured the first cup and knocked on Marcus's bedroom door. There was no immediate answer, so she knocked again a little louder. Still no response. She became aware of the sound of running water from one of the bathrooms, and, presuming that was where he was, Alex opened the door quietly and went in to put the cup of tea on the bedside table.

She had gone in without hesitation, so it was a shock when she saw that Marcus was still in bed, lying on his front, his face turned towards her and one arm flung up

148

His grey eyes looked steadily into hers. 'It occurred to me that with your need for a job and the comparatively pleasant easiness of this one you might be inclined to see this week as an opportunity to get ahead of the opposition. Thinking along those lines would not be a good idea.'

Alex stared at him in outrage. 'Do you really think me capable of scheming like that?'

'Your sister seemed to keep her mind firmly on her own interests. It may be a family characteristic you share.'

'Thinking like that reflects more discredit on you than on me,' she said passionately, but keeping her voice low out of concern for Becky. 'I wouldn't consider working here permanently for a king's ransom. In fact, after a start to the day like this, I'm beginning to wonder why on earth I offered to stay on at all.'

The door was suddenly pushed open. 'Hi, everybody!' Becky's bright voice said. 'Here you all are!'

She was in her pants and vest, her thin legs braced by the clumsy-looking calipers, but her face shining bright and eager.

'I take that back,' Alex said softly. 'There's my reason.' Then, walking away from him, she said, 'Morning, Becky,' in a completely different tone.

Becky caught her hand. 'Alex, Uncle Marcus—I won't be such a nuisance again, I promise, but Mistral's been here twelve hours now, and I haven't ridden her properly with my own saddle and everything. So can we go out . . . quickly?'

Alex saw Marcus's face change as he greeted his small niece. 'What an impatient sprog you are! We shall have to see whether Alex can bear the thought of riding before breakfast.'

'Don't count me in,' Alex said firmly, flashing him a look that said nothing could appeal to her less than staying a moment longer in his company. 'I shall make breakfast while you two go out.' She ruffled Becky's dark hair. 'Then when you come back ravenous everything will be ready.'

'You'd better go and put some clothes on, Becky. Have you washed properly?' Marcus asked the child. She was bobbing up and down in excitement.

'Oh, Uncle Marcus! Of course I have. I've been washing myself properly for *ages* now.'

'Run along, then.' Alex was following Becky, but he called her back again. 'Just a minute, Alex.'

'I would have thought everything had been said that needs to be said,' she told him, still smarting from his attitude of only moments ago.

He swung his long legs out of bed, and hitched up the black silk pyjama trousers he was wearing, standing then with his hands on his hips, looking at her.

'Perhaps a little too much was said. My experience of your sex has caused me to suspect everyone's motives. If I was wrong and your feelings are hurt, I apologise.'

'I assure you there's no need to confuse me with my sister,' Alex said unrelentingly. 'When this week is up, you won't need to tell me to go. I'll be on my way, and not a minute too soon.'

'If you choose to brush aside an apology, so be it,' he said, apparently unconcerned. 'Changing the subject, as far as the riding goes, I wasn't suggesting you come with us for a social outing. I want to show you the best routes to take, then I'll know you and Becky are all right together when I'm otherwise engaged. So I'd be glad if you would conquer your displeasure and come along.'

'As always, you're the boss,' Alex said stonily, and left his room, closing the door behind her with exemplary gentleness while feeling she would like to slam it in his face.

You knew he was like this, she told herself angrily while she dressed. From the moment you heard Elaine crying down the phone, you knew what kind of a man

Marcus Wakeford was, but like a fool you had to find out for yourself.

But behind the anger was deep hurt that a man who could look at Becky with such tenderness should have such a different set of expressions for her. And still she had this desperate longing for him to love her. She had no shame, no pride, no loyalty to family. Just a crippling, humiliating desire to be loved.

The fresh air and Becky's infectious enthusiasm for the ride did something to make Alex forget her hurt. It was difficult to remain miserable on the smiling Downs under the forget-me-not blue of the sky.

Marcus was riding a big bay, Alex was on Lasco, and Becky was covering twice as much ground as the two of them on Mistral. She had quickly learned the degree of control the little horse required, and now she came cantering back towards them to circle and fall in between them with a sunny smile at each.

'Isn't this lovely?' she said, riding along sedately for a moment. 'We're like Mummy Bear, Daddy Bear and Baby Bear. A real family.' Then she was off at a canter again, leaving Alex smiling cynically at the innocent words, and Marcus frowning, she saw.

'Perhaps I should have prepared you for that particular attitude,' he said.

Alex stiffened. 'You don't think I'm in danger of taking what a child says seriously. Come on, Marcus! It was a thoughtless, childish remark. She didn't mean it.'

'I wouldn't be so sure about that. Becky has been on the marriage trail on my behalf more than once. She's not to know how particularly inappropriate the idea would be in this case.'

He was saying nothing she did not know herself, but his cold statement of the facts still wounded.

'Don't worry. I'll make sure she knows my interest is involved with someone else,' she said curtly.

'Becky may appear older than her years in some ways,' he went on, doggedly pursuing his theme, 'but she's the only one at her school without a mother and that makes her vulnerable. It's a blank she's determined I shall fill—and that's one reason why I wasn't keen for you to stay on. Apart from any assumptions on her part being distasteful to you, they could end by hurting Becky.'

'I think you've made quite sure that I'll be aware of the situation,' Alex said coldly. 'But what about Anna? Doesn't she get considered for the role?'

'Anna's twice your age. More of a grandmother. And she doesn't care for horses.' He looked sidelong at her. 'Unfortunately, you—I imagine—come close to a child's ideal. Young, pretty, a rider, and, to crown it all, someone who appears like fairy-tale magic from the sea with a white Camargue horse.'

'I expect Becky will gradually learn that marriage depends on two people finding each other acceptable.'

'I expect she will,' he replied expressionlessly. 'And that's an entirely different can of worms from a child's fairy-story, as we well know. We'd better catch her up. She's getting too far ahead of us.'

In every way, Alex's bitter inward voice added.

The first chance for Alex to establish her 'otherwise involved' status came when Marcus suggested a drive to a favourite teashop later that day for Sunday afternoon cakes.

'I'll stay here, if you don't mind,' she said casually, knowing that Becky was looking expectantly at her. 'I want to write to Ambrose.'

'Who's Ambrose?' the child asked, instantly alert.

'My boyfriend.'

'I don't like his name,' Becky said forthrightly.

'Becky, that's rude,' Marcus warned sternly.

'Sorry. May I see his picture?'

'I'm afraid I haven't got one,' Alex was forced to admit. 'I didn't have a lot of room in my holiday luggage.'

There was the briefest pause. 'Why didn't he go on holiday with you?'

Alex was beginning to believe Marcus's assessment of the diminutive creature now grilling her as 'older than her years'.

'Doctors can't always have a holiday when they want one,' she said.

'Didn't he want you to wait until he could go to the seaside too?'

'Becky,' Marcus said, coming to the rescue, 'if you go on asking questions much longer we shan't get our cakes and Ambrose won't get his letter.' He took the child's hand and firmly led her towards the door, his glance at Alex saying, Didn't I tell you?

Later that night after Becky had gone to bed, he broached the subject of payment, which angered Alex as she had intended her offer of help to be just that, not an extension of paid work.

'I offered to help out as a friend,' she said, regretting the word as soon as she had spoken it.

'You know perfectly well that I can't allow you to do that.' It sounded as though he was pointing out how impossible it was for him to consider her in that light. She flushed with embarrassment.

'Then pay me whatever you think appropriate for a servant,' she told him tersely.

'Of course I don't regard you as a servant——' he began.

'I don't want to talk about it,' she flung at him. 'Make your own mind up since you have created the problem. Don't expect me to negotiate like a shop steward.'

He looked freezingly at her. 'I see you are determined to be as difficult as possible.'

'Only as difficult as you force me to be.' This time it could not be said that she closed the door gently.

It was as well, she decided, that Marcus had such a busy week. She saw little of him. He ate out and came in usually after she had gone to bed. But on the rare times when they did meet without Becky's softening influence, the atmosphere between them was no better.

The house itself wove a spell round her. Chessetts dated from 1785, that much she knew from the date stone over the front door. The house had the nooks and crannies and steps up and down that created the charm of an old property, and it was furnished delightfully. The big, squashy chairs and sofas with their loose covers had been chosen for comfort, but the items of antique furniture looked as though they had been selected for love of the craftsmanship that had gone into their making. Marcus's study had shelves of modern novels as well as the classics, and Alex couldn't help noticing that, however great their differences, they shared a taste for several crime writers. There was a silver-framed photograph on his desk, and the inscription identified the smiling couple in it as Becky's parents.

Alex stood looking at them, saddened at the thought of such laughing enjoyment of life being no more. At least they could rest assured that their daughter was being well taken care of. No uncle could feel more genuine affection for his niece than Marcus felt for Becky. However much Alex might hold against him, she certainly had to grant him that.

She loved the house, and however hopelessly, however irrationally, she loved the man. She spent the hours when she was on her own performing small tasks that unwittingly were evidence of this—flowers in his study, tempting supper trays that as often as not were left untouched, clothes beautifully laundered.

'Playing the wife, are you?' she asked herself scornfully when she realised what she was doing. 'Fool! Traitor! Shameless idiot!' And on Wednesday night she deliberately left no supper tray.

Perversely he came in before she had gone to bed, and she was forced to offer to make him something.

'Something easy, if you don't mind. A sandwich.' He flung himself into a chair after switching on *Newsnight* and she went off to the kitchen to cut slices from a new granary loaf and fill them with chicken.

'Stay and drink it with me,' he said, sounding for once as though he meant it, when she had poured coffee and picked up her own cup to take upstairs with her.

'All right. Just for a moment or two.' She sat down warily on the edge of her chair.

'Becky all right?'

'She's fine. Fast asleep now.'

'I'll look in on her when I go up to wash the city dust off. Did she do her homework?'

'It was a bit of a joint effort. Sums.'

He smiled. 'Wednesday's usually a bad day. Good old Becky.'

Newsnight caught their attention for a moment or two, and when Alex glanced across at him she saw that Marcus's eyes were closed. He looked very tired, and, as on that first morning when she had been watching him sleeping, his guard was down. He was still holding his coffee-cup in one hand, tilting at a dangerous angle.

Her heart filling with loving concern for him, she got up and gently attempted to take it from him.

The long eyelashes fluttered and opened, and he gave her a smile of such unexpectedly genuine warmth that her foolish, eager heart began pounding. No...she told herself sharply. It means nothing. You're someone in a dream, that's all.

'Sorry,' he said. 'It's been a hard day. It's strange to open my eyes and find you here. Not very complimentary to have them closed, though.'

'Being complimentary isn't something that has featured strongly on the agenda between us, is it?' Alex said quietly.

He seized her wrist, the smile disappearing and his eyes flashing dangerously. 'You never miss a damned trick, do you?'

She concentrated on not reacting to his touch. 'I can't help being realistic. More coffee?'

He let her go, his face wiping clean of feeling and closing to her. 'I'll help myself when you've gone up.'

He might as well say, That will be all, Alexandra, she thought with the miserable satisfaction of having been right. The genuine smile hadn't lasted for more than seconds. The vicious feeling of his grip on her wrist would last far longer.

'Anyone phone?' he said as she reached the door.

'No. I made one call to my parents.'

'You don't have to report on every phone call you make,' he said irritably. His eyes narrowed. 'Did you tell them where you were?'

'I didn't go into details,' she said shortly.

'Don't you wish you'd taken better care of your money? Losing it hasn't made life easy for you.'

'Or you,' she said, meeting his eyes. 'Anyway, whoever said life was easy?'

'My experience so far hasn't proved it so.'

It was as close as they had come to agreement in all the time they had spent together.

Alex drove into Eastbourne next day and got herself a selection of publications advertising her kind of job. She had to do something to draw her mind towards the real future instead of dwelling on a mythical impossible one. She had taken paper and envelopes with her, and sat in a sea-front café to send off a couple of applications. There was no sense of happy looking forward when she had done so, only a dreary feeling of satisfaction that she had taken this small step.

Marcus came in that night just before Becky went to bed. He had a paper bag which he put in the little girl's hands with the words, 'Something you've been coveting, I think.'

Becky opened the bag excitedly and gave a shout of delight as she pulled out a pair of pyjamas with a mouse on the front.

'Oh, great, Uncle Marcus!' she exclaimed gleefully. 'Look, Alex—just like yours!' She scrambled up and flung her arms round Marcus. 'They're lovely! Thank you. I'll wear them tonight. I'm going to put them on now.'

She went off upstairs as quickly as she could, and Marcus brought out another bag and put it on the table in front of Alex. 'This is for you. A token of appreciation, if you like.'

With some misgivings Alex opened her parcel. A creation in silk and lace came tumbling out—the most stunningly seductive pale green nightdress anyone could wish to see. But Alex stared at it as though a snake had slithered out of the bag.

A token of appreciation? The nightdress didn't proclaim itself as such to her. What was there about her that he appreciated? He couldn't stand her! Was this his way of saying that as a person she was impossible, but the shape of her, the look of her—well, at least she was decorative? It was that sort of nightdress. She turned eyes glittering with protest on Marcus.

'What's this?'

'I'm sick of seeing that damned mouse crawling across your chest,' he said carelessly, sitting down opposite her. 'You've been wearing it ever since we left the Camargue. It's time it had a wash, anyway.'

'Of course my pyjamas have been washed,' Alex said scathingly. 'I've got two pairs exactly the same.'

'Then it's high time you had a change, isn't it?'

She put the soft, beautiful—but, to her, offensive—garment back into its bag and pushed it over the table towards him.

The look of something akin to satisfaction that had been on his face faded.

'What am I to understand by that?'

'That I don't accept your gift.' Her voice rose in accusation. 'You must have known how inappropriate it was to give me something like this.'

'For heaven's sake!' he exclaimed. 'Stop reading penny-novelettish significance into it. I saw both things in a shop window and bought them on impulse. There was neither ulterior meaning nor motive.'

'I went to great lengths outside school today to correct Becky's description of me to her friend Emma as "living with Uncle Marcus". If an account of that sort of gift gets round school, it would be all the same if I'd saved my breath.'

He looked scathingly at her. 'Does it really matter so much what a bunch of schoolkids babble about?'

'It seemed to matter very much to you that one particular schoolkid shouldn't get any wrong ideas. If Becky's so smart, isn't she going to take a present like this as a very matey gesture indeed?'

In an outburst of temper he swiped at the packet on the table and sent it flying into Alex's lap. 'It's a matter of complete indifference to me what you do with the thing. Fly it from the hospital flagpole, send it to the local jumble sale, give it to the dustmen.'

'Don't imagine I won't!' Alex said, holding the bag as though it were an unexploded bomb as she headed for the door.

'Suit yourself. I made a mistake. I hadn't got you down as someone with the mind of a Victorian tweeny.'

'Think what you like,' she said, her voice practically breaking with anger. Then she remembered something, not unconnected. 'I'm glad to say Anna phoned this afternoon. She'll be back on Saturday.'

'Thank God for that!'

'Exactly!' She went off upstairs, determined not to appear from her room again that night.

She heard Marcus come up and speak to Becky in her room, then go down and shut himself in his study. Only then did she feel relaxed enough to begin packing the things she wouldn't need again, most of which went into her bag sprinkled with the tears of miserable reaction she was shedding.

She had washed and dried her hair and was about to take off the green Paisley dressing gown and get into bed when there was a soft knock on her bedroom door.

Hurriedly Alex switched off the light and held her breath.

'It's no good pretending to be asleep,' Marcus's voice said softly. 'I saw the light. Come on, Alex.'

Reluctantly she went and opened the door and told him, 'I was just about to get into bed.'

'Look,' he said, 'that was a ridiculous quarrel. Not worth going to bed on. I've just made some tea. Come and have a cup.'

She must have looked as doubtful as she felt.

'You have my word that I'll behave perfectly,' he said, and, though she looked hard at him to find any trace of mockery in his expression, there was none.

'All right, then,' she said slowly, and followed him down the stairs. I'm like a dog that's been kicked, she told herself. One soft word from the master, and I'm running straight for the next humiliation.

In the kitchen he poured the tea and pushed a plate of chocolate biscuits towards her.

'Peace offering. I really didn't mean to upset you. Perhaps I could have chosen a less personal gift. I just saw the nightdress in the window and thought instantly that it was exactly your colour. There was nothing more to it than that.'

As she looked into the grey eyes, now holding her own so kindly, Alex felt her wariness melting like snow in summer. 'I expect I overdid the reaction. I—I can't deny that it's a beautiful thing.' Somehow the word 'nightdress' was impossible to say and too emotive by far. To her horror, as she spoke her hand began to shake and her voice to do likewise. What on earth was the matter with her? She put her cup down and turned away, ready for flight.

'Alex——' He stepped to the other side of her and prevented her leaving. His expression was suddenly as tender as the one on his face when he looked at Becky, and its effect was to make her give a loud, gulping sob. She scrubbed at her eyes with the sleeve of her robe.

'I don't know what's happening to me. Temper one minute, and tears the next.'

He was reaching out towards her, and she couldn't bear to be touched. If he touched her she would be drawn like a magnet to cling to him and cry even more and make an even greater fool of herself than she was already doing. All he felt was momentary sympathy, perhaps with a fair old measure of normal male reaction to a half-dressed female.

She stepped back hurriedly. 'But I expect tears and tantrums are par for the course when a Leeward and a Wakeford get together,' she said, turning back to pick up her teacup.

'Damn the Leewards! Damn the Wakefords!' he said, his expression changing so swiftly that it was almost comical—if anyone had felt like laughing.

'I think I'll take my tea upstairs.' Her unnaturally sparkling eyes met his just as a tear spilled over and ran down her cheek. 'Before the peace offering becomes a weapon of war.'

'Go on, then. Run away!' he said viciously. 'For one moment I actually thought you were going to forget who you are.'

'I don't think either of us is capable of doing that, Marcus,' she said.

He folded his arms and watched her go. When she reached the door she heard him give a bitter laugh.

'So much for perfect behaviour,' floated up the stairs after her.

With dogged determination, Marcus informed her next day that he was determined not to part on bad terms. He was going to take the afternoon off, so that they could collect Becky from school and go and picnic at Birling Gap. Only a small picnic, because he intended taking the pair of them out for a meal in the evening. Alex protested that he didn't have to do that, to which he replied that he knew he didn't, but he was damned well going to. Considering it when he had gone, she thought that it was all to the good that Becky should be around for most of the evening. The child's presence would help her own self-control, and ensure that of Marcus.

The picnic was fine, though Alex thought her heart would break as she watched Marcus and Becky investigating one of the rock pools. They could both be so dear to her if only... She thought that the image of them under the dazzling chalk faces of the Seven Sisters would stay in her mind to torture her with dreams of what might have been for the rest of her life.

They were getting ready for the meal out when Marcus came to Alex's room to say that Becky was not well. She felt sick and wanted to go to bed.

'Then we must cancel the table for tonight,' Alex told him. 'There's cold meat in the refrigerator.'

'Becky doesn't want that. In fact she even phoned Mrs Ellerton before she told me she was unwell, and arranged for her to baby-sit. She says she didn't want to spoil the fun.'

Alex was taken aback by such initiative. In fact she was frankly suspicious of it, she decided after a moment. 'I don't at all mind staying here,' she said, thinking at the same time it wasn't going to be an easy evening.

'But Becky would mind—very much.' He looked at her black dress, at the shining copper hair piled on her head, at the Italian shawl trailing from one hand. 'No. You're all ready. I think we'll go ahead as planned. There's nothing wrong with Becky that early bed won't cure.'

'If you're happy to do that . . .'

'I'm not exactly happy about anything. It's a matter of choosing the lesser of two evils,' he said flatly, turning to go downstairs.

Alex's suspicions about Becky's motives deepened when she went in to say goodnight. A face that looked decidedly normal lit up at the sight of Alex's appearance. 'Uncle Marcus will like that!' she said of the black dress. 'It's quite bare, isn't it?'

There was no point in saying anything, though, Alex decided. Tomorrow it would all be over and Becky would settle down with Anna again.

Neither she nor Marcus was finding the evening easy, she thought as she met his eyes across the table in the charming old-world country-house hotel he had taken her to. The panelled alcove in which they were sitting was meant for intimacy, but neither of them seemed to have their minds on the brittle, superficial conversation that was the best they could manage. Alex was having great difficulty in coping with her food, delicious though it was, and both of them had declined a dessert from the magnificent trolley brought to the table.

She made a determined effort and raised her glass. 'Here's to a trouble-free future, Marcus.'

He lifted his own glass in a token gesture. 'I'll drink to that, but without much faith in miracles, no matter how much a child like Becky and a man with businesses to run could do with them.'

Her eyes lowered, Alex asked, 'Have you never considered doing what Becky would like—marrying?'

She felt the silence become almost electric, to be broken by the snapping of the stem of Marcus's empty glass as his hand clenched around it. He seemed unaware of what he had done.

'I only meant that it would be so much easier for you...' she said lamely. 'Becky's right about that.'

'Is that what marriage means to you?' he said fiercely. 'Life made easy? All the problems ironed out?'

'You're twisting a perfectly innocent question.' But was it innocent? What answer had her subconscious been hoping for?

'Then let me reply to your innocent question with a cynical answer. I quickly learned that your sex is far from dreamy-eyed when it comes to marriage. A man with an attractive house and bank balance is fair game—but a man with all that and a little niece who may need more care than the average child—no go. To quote your own words, not even "a king's ransom" would make the prospect appealing. A week is as much as anyone can take. One or two encounters with that sort of attitude quickly put a man off the so-called fair sex. Becky and I will do very well on our own. But enough about me. Let's talk about someone who has organised her life very advantageously. Tell me, how *is* Elaine these days?'

She was shocked that he should mention her sister's name with such sarcasm in his voice. Shocked even more that in the context of the conversation they had been having he should hark back to the end of that particular relationship. She answered him very briefly.

'She's fine.'

'One of the lucky ones who has found a suitable partner?'

'Yes. And you've already commented on that. I don't think there's anything to be gained from discussing my sister, do you, Marcus?'

'I'm glad to know she's happy. You can't find fault with that, surely?'

'Elaine's happiness ceased to be any concern of yours some time ago.' Alex was outraged that he should be so lacking in taste as to discuss the feelings of the girl he had so ruthlessly discarded.

'And yet you still seem to bear a grudge against *me* for what happened over two years ago.' His eyes held hers, refusing to let her look away. 'I find that strange.'

Alex's anger rose, colouring her cheeks, making her eyes blaze. 'Strange? If things hadn't happened as they did between you and Elaine, she would still be in this country. How do you expect us to feel? She's my only sister, and I hardly ever see her. My parents have a grandchild who will scarcely know them.'

'The fact that Elaine felt she had to run away was hardly my fault. If she couldn't cope with what happened, it was down to her. I'm still around.'

Alex couldn't believe what she was hearing. How could he speak like this? Only the fact that they were among a crowd of people prevented her losing control of herself. With a superhuman effort she spoke quietly.

'I'm not going to discuss what happened between you and Elaine.' She scraped back her chair. 'I'd like to go home, Marcus.'

'Don't you mean you'd like to go back to Chessetts?' he said, his eyes cold as winter. 'Very well. Tonight was a mistake. This whole week has been a mistake. The biggest mistake of all was my ever giving credence to the idea that it could possibly work for you to take Liz's place.'

He stood and came round to pull out her chair.

'I agree.' She struggled to salvage politeness from the wreck of the evening. 'Nevertheless, thank you for the meal.'

'Supper in a condemned cell might have had the edge on it,' he said grimly as they left the table.

As she got out of the car at Chessetts, Alex trod on a pebble and turned the slender heel of her shoe. She fell against Marcus, and the sudden contact was her undoing...the undoing, it seemed, of both of them.

In an instant Marcus's arms were round her and the feeble protest she would have made was silenced by his mouth crushing hers. Alex was powerless as the blood in her veins, the heart and soul of her rose to match his need.

He tore his lips from hers for a second. 'Don't talk!' he said savagely, and in the moonlight she saw that his eyes were dark, and felt his body taut with desire. 'What use are words to us? Words do nothing but divide us, when I know that behind all the words is this...' Then he was kissing her again, and the fire of response was blazing through her, her lips and her hands and her body as eager as his.

He paused, breathing hard, and buried his face in her hair as though he wanted to eat her. 'From the start you've driven me mad,' he panted. 'I've fought you and berated you and told myself I hated you, but underneath it all I've wanted nothing more than to make love to you. And you feel it too, Alex. You can't deny it. I see it in your eyes, hear it in your voice, sense it like an aura round your body when I come near to you.'

His head came down so that he could kiss her shoulder. The strap of her flimsy dress was pushed impatiently aside. She was sinking under a welter of feelings that could only lead to a situation that would cause her even more unhappiness.

'Marcus——' Using all her strength, she pushed against his pounding chest, making him look at her. 'It's no use,' she said, her voice choked. 'The words are there, whether we speak them or not. The reason that separated you and Elaine is just as much there between you and me. This is——' she sought the word '—it's nothing more than madness. And when the madness dies, the words will be waiting to make themselves heard. Nothing will have changed.'

His arms tightened round her and his eyes burned into hers. 'Can you say that, here, now, so close to me? Can't you feel how much I want you?'

'What does it matter if I say it or not?' she asked him brokenly. 'Spoken or unspoken, the situation that keeps us apart is not going to go away. We both know that.'

It was as though she watched him die as she saw the urgent passion leave his face, saw the lines of harsh control return and his eyes lose their light.

At that moment the door opened as far as the safety chain would allow and a shaft of bright light fell on the drive. Mrs Ellerton's voice called tentatively, 'Is that you, Mr Wakeford?'

Alex shrank back behind the sweet cascade of blossoming wistaria. 'I can't face her——' she breathed, panic-stricken.

Marcus was in control of himself and the situation once more, and it was as though the fierce, burning man of moments ago had ceased to exist as he said calmly, going towards the door, 'Yes, Mrs Ellerton. Alex has just gone over to check the horses. Everything all right? Ready for a lift home?'

She heard their voices die away into the house, and soundlessly pushed further into the shrubbery at the side of Chessetts. Not until they came out and got into the car and drove away into the night did she move again, then she went silently indoors, past her dishevelled white reflection in the hall mirror and up the stairs to her room, knowing that she had taken as much as she could and reached breaking point. She had to get away, not subject herself to one more moment's torture with Marcus.

She finished her packing, creeping around quietly in her room, a prey to the worst misery she had ever experienced. Marcus came in and went straight to his own bed. After that, knowing she wouldn't sleep a wink, Alex sat by the window in the dark with tears sliding slowly down her cheeks, waiting for the first light to appear on the horizon. When the brightness was halfway across the sky, she went with cautious, leaden footsteps down the stairs. No one heard her. She took the Metro she had been driving all week, leaving a note to Marcus explaining that she could think of no other way of getting to the station, and telling him that he would find the car in the station car park. She wrote another note to Becky, saying that she hated goodbyes, and saying goodbye to her would have been especially painful. She promised to write soon, a letter just for Becky, addressed to her.

Then with one last look at the lovely old house she drove off, the pain of leaving beyond tears, beyond words, making her heart heavy as a huge stone in her chest . . .

CHAPTER NINE

ALEX let herself into the house after paying off the taxi that had brought her to her parents' home from the first train to Kingston-by-Sea. No one seemed to be around. Her father would be playing the leisurely round of golf his doctor encouraged him to enjoy a cautious once a week. Then a flurry of splashing sounds from upstairs made it clear that Mrs Leeward was in the bath. Seeing her white face and darkly shadowed eyes, Alex was glad to have time to get a cup of coffee inside her before she had to put on an 'all's well' act for her mother.

The phone rang just as the kettle boiled, and she picked up the receiver, automatically repeating the number.

'So that's where you are,' Marcus's voice said in her ear.

She put the phone down with as much revulsion as though she had picked up a snake by mistake. She couldn't—she *could not* speak to him. Enough was enough. Quickly she switched on the answering machine, only just in time, for again the phone shrilled out, and after the routine three rings Marcus's voice, not quite so cool this time, spoke clearly in the sunlit kitchen.

'Alex—it's obvious that you've reached home safely, though you might have been considerate enough to let us know. I have to speak to you about the money owing to you. Please pick up the phone. All I need is the number of your bank account, so stop this ridiculous game and allow matters to be settled sensibly.'

Money... That was all he was concerned about. Employer and employee. Hurt beyond belief that money was the only matter remaining to be settled between

170

them, she switched off the answering machine. If he wanted to talk about money, she could just about manage to make her opinion known on that subject. More calmly now, but at what cost only she knew, Alex picked up the phone when it rang again, and listened to his, 'That's better——' before cutting in,

'I don't want any further conversation with you, Marcus. You must realise how inappropriate it is for you to ring my parents' home. And I don't want your money. There are some things that simply cannot be paid for, and this past week was one of them. Please don't contact me again.'

Then, without giving him a second's chance to reply, she replaced the receiver for a moment before removing it again and leaving it hanging from the wall.

Somehow the money issue put last night into perspective. All Marcus had been acknowledging in those now unbelievable moments outside Chessetts was that there was undeniable sexual attraction between them. But that was not love. A man who loved would not have been so cruel as to suggest that a cheque paid into her bank account could 'settle matters'. Thank God Mrs Ellerton had called from the door when she had. The sight of Marcus's face, that draining of life she had watched, had almost succeeded in making Alex take back every word she had spoken. But she knew now that she had watched nothing more serious than the frustrated disappointment of an aroused man. Today he was ready to pay her off and forget her.

Mrs Leeward took one look at her daughter's pale, tense face when she came downstairs, and chatted comfortably while she made breakfast her first priority. When Alex was sipping her coffee and nibbling half-heartedly at a piece of toast, her mother gently asked, 'Has it been a hard week, then? You don't exactly look like someone coming home from a good holiday.'

'Only hard because I didn't get on with the man I was working for,' Alex said, avoiding her mother's eyes. 'It was a case of a constant clash of personalities. Not the easiest of circumstances.'

'Then why on earth did you agree to stay on for another week once you were back in England?' Mrs Leeward asked, not unreasonably.

'Because I sympathised with the staff problem he found waiting for him. I didn't have to like him to do that. And the little girl I was looking after was a sweetie. Anyway, it's over now. Let's forget about it.'

Mrs Leeward knew Alex well, and was sure that there was more to it than her daughter was willing to admit. But she recognised the determined tone of voice, and asked no further questions.

When Mr Leeward came in from golf, looking much fitter, Alex saw, he was more concerned with scolding her for not letting him know about her financial difficulties in the Camargue than with questioning her about the days that had followed. Alex told him that she had not wanted to worry him, and reminded him that she was old enough to sort out her own problems, then turned the conversation to her search for a new post.

During the next few days she coped well on the surface and in daylight. But at night she had nightmare after nightmare, all of them linked to Marcus Wakeford but focusing at first on other people caught up in the situation. Sometimes it was her sister, not the happy wife and mother of reality, but a weak, fading shadow of herself, reproaching Alex for caring so little about her that she could imagine love for the man who had caused so much hurt. Sometimes it was her father, suddenly made aware of his second daughter's treachery, clutching his heart, his face contorted with pain.

One night she had the worst nightmare of all. She was on one side of a yawning chasm that was growing wider and deeper every second. On the other side of it was

Marcus, being carried further and further away from her by the greedily growing pit that separated them. The utter desolation she felt as she watched him disappear into the shadows and realised how impossible it was for her to get to him was unbearable.

She must have cried out in her sleep, because when she came to her senses she found her bedside light on, her mother bending over her.

'Alex,' she said in loving concern, sitting down on the bed, 'what's giving you these bad dreams? This isn't the first time you've cried out with such distress in your sleep. Is there something you would feel better for telling me?'

Night and nightmare brought vulnerability. Once she had made sure that her father was still fast asleep, Alex told her mother everything, and found some kind of temporary relief in sharing the knowledge that was putting her through such subconscious torture. Mrs Leeward listened in silence after her initial incredulity that Marcus Wakeford and Alex should have been brought together in such a strange way, her face for the rest of the story calm, sympathetic, attentive. Alex concluded with the stumbling words, 'I must be the biggest fool in creation. He made no secret of the disgust he felt when he found out that I was Elaine's sister. He never let me feel for one moment that he could forget that I was one of the hated Leewards ... and yet I went on and on wanting it to be different between us.'

'We don't choose who to love,' Mrs Leeward said quietly. 'If we fall in love with someone who is suitable, never mind eligible, and who—miracle of miracles—actually loves us in return, then we are truly the lucky ones.'

'But someone who had caused my father to be so ill!'

'Marcus Wakeford wasn't the sole bearer of that responsibility,' her mother said firmly. 'Elaine played games and lost. Your father had been warned by his doctor for several years to take things easy, but he went on overworking. And, though it can be said that Marcus

Wakeford's reaction when he found out about Elaine's deception triggered off events, that wretched coronary had been threatening for years—and the ground had been well prepared by generations of Leewards and Wakefords with their wretched quarrel.' Her voice was impatient. 'It's high time that old feud was forgotten. It's caused enough damage over the years.'

'Try telling that to Marcus,' Alex said miserably, scrubbing at her damp face with a tissue. 'It's alive and flourishing in his mind.' She made an effort to pull herself together. 'But now that I've burdened you with the shameful secret, perhaps I can begin to make myself forget it. I've got an interview tomorrow. That's one good thing to look forward to.'

'One thing of many, my love,' her mother said with conviction.

Alex got the job, a temporary replacement for someone recovering from a sporting injury, but it was something to do, something to occupy her thoughts until a permanent post was found.

She exchanged a couple of letters with Becky, telling herself that the correspondence would die a natural death on the little girl's side before long. Becky's endearingly misspelled letter was full of Mistral and a forthcoming gymkhana, the first in which they were to take part. There was only a passing reference to Marcus, who was 'very bizzy' in Becky language.

There were plenty of people ready to be friendly at her new hospital, and Alex resolutely accepted most of the social invitations she received. No sudden miracle happened. Her heart still didn't seem to be fully in anything she did. Sometimes she could almost see the ghost of Marcus superimposed on the person across the dinner-table or partnering her on the squash court. And every fair male head she saw was an instant reminder of him. But she was filling her time and enjoyment of life would no doubt come in due course, she told herself.

One night, while she was still at her parents' home, since there was no point in moving until she had a permanent job, she was surprised to answer the phone and hear Becky's voice on the end of the line.

'Becky! How lovely to hear you!' Alex said. In reality it was both pleasure and pain as she pictured the hall at Chessetts, knowing the table on which the phone stood, and the chair on which Becky was no doubt kneeling. Was Marcus somewhere there, listening?

The child had a request to make, and went straight into it.

'Alex, it's the gymkhana on Saturday, and Uncle Marcus has a silly old business meeting. I do want someone who knows Mistral to watch us. Do you think you might be able to come? Please!'

Alex heard the intense pleading in the young voice, and could imagine Becky's disappointment that her beloved uncle wouldn't see her ride. But going back into Becky's orbit herself was something she thought it unwise to do. A sniff and a gulp down the line tore at her heart, though.

'Is your uncle there now?' she asked cautiously.

'No. He's over with the horses. I do want somebody who cares to be there. Please, Alex.'

'I expect Anna will be cheering you on, won't she?'

'Yes...' the voice was doubtful '...but she doesn't really know Mistral. Not like you do. It's our first gymkhana, Alex.'

'I think you shouldn't be doing this, though I do understand your disappointment,' Alex said gently.

'Anyone can come to the field. You pay at the gate. It doesn't cost much, honestly. And it isn't very far for you, is it? I looked on the map.'

There was an expectant silence.

'Please...' the quivering voice urged. 'We've got the date for me to go into hospital again...'

What harm could it really do? Alex asked herself. Marcus wouldn't be there. And it obviously meant so much to Becky to have someone around who had been in on the Mistral story from the start. But it wouldn't do to establish a precedent.

'Perhaps just this once, since it's your first ride...' she stressed, the words barely uttered before there was a cheer down the phone.

'Oh, thanks a million, million times, Alex. It's in a field beside the road and there will be big signs.' She broke into an excited description of exactly where the gymkhana was to be held, stressing the time the events were scheduled to start. Then with a repeated flurry of thank-yous the call ended.

Not wise, Alex reproached herself. But it was done now. She wouldn't go back on her word. However, she wouldn't let herself be caught on the hop again.

Saturday afternoon was gloriously sunny. Alex wore a burnt sugar linen dress with flat matching sandals suitable for the field, and tied back her glowing hair with a striped black, copper and gold scarf. The gymkhana field was buzzing with pre-event activity when she arrived and parked her elderly Mini. She wandered through the crowds of parents, ponies and children, looking for Mistral's white coat and mane.

She spotted her at last at the far end of the field. Becky was immaculate in riding jacket and hat, her specially adapted jodhpurs covering her 'second legs' as she called her calipers. She was giving a last-minute touch to Mistral's already perfect mane, watched by a motherly-looking woman, presumably Anna, whose face revealed a little of the anxiety Marcus had told Alex they all felt in case Becky had a fall. Alex's heart warmed with real affection for the brave little girl.

'Hello, rider!' she called joyfully when she was within earshot.

Becky spun round and flung herself into Alex's arms.

'Thank you for coming!' she said fiercely, then in an urgent undertone, 'You won't be cross, will you?'

Alex wondered momentarily what was meant by this strange greeting, but then, over Becky's shoulder, she had the shattering explanation. A familiar tall male figure was coming round the corner of the horse-box, someone with a shining cap of dark gold hair, grey eyes that were looking at her with a quickly masked expression of total shock. Alex felt as though the blood had stopped dead in her veins.

Becky was hanging on to her hand like a leech.

'I forgot to tell you, Uncle Marcus,' she said with only the slightest quiver in her voice, 'I asked Alex to come and see me ride today.'

'A strange thing to forget,' Marcus said ominously, but he held out his hand towards Alex with admirable control. 'Good afternoon, Alex. This is a surprise.'

At least he didn't go so far as to use the qualifying adjective 'pleasant'. Well, it wasn't for her either. It was an absolute stunner of a shock.

What had happened to the meeting that was supposedly preventing his attendance here today? She caught Becky's eye and saw a flash of guilt—defiant guilt, but guilt none the less. Damn it—there had probably never been a meeting at all. She had been duped by a scheming seven-year-old who would end up in an all-woman gaol at this rate of progress. Her eyes returned their own message to Becky, but it would have to remain unspoken for the time being.

'You haven't met Anna, have you?' Marcus was saying smoothly, carrying out the process of introduction as though it were a perfectly normal meeting.

'I've heard a lot about you,' Anna said, the only one of them to be truly at ease. 'Becky hasn't stopped talking about you since you left. It was so good of you to step in and cope with the emergency.'

Alex found her voice. 'How is your sister now? It must have been a very worrying time.'

'She's improving steadily. I shall be seeing her tomorrow to make sure all's well.'

There was a feeling of total unreality in the air. Alex couldn't believe that she had been so foolish as to risk something like this. If there was a next step after frying-pan and fire, then this was it. How on earth was she to get through this afternoon? She couldn't turn round and leave, but that was what it would be such a relief to do now, with Marcus's politeness hiding the intense displeasure that was obvious to her, if not to Anna, displeasure that would erupt at some point. Nothing was more certain than that.

A voice over the Tannoy called riders in the first event to the starting point and Becky thankfully disappeared, followed by Anna who said she wanted to have a word with Becky's friend Emma's mother. Alex's heart gave a drum-roll of apprehension at the thought of being left alone with Marcus. Tension was almost screaming in the air between them.

'You shouldn't have come,' Marcus said suddenly, the cutting coldness of his voice making Alex jump. 'What on earth was the point?'

'Do you think I would have done if I'd known you were going to be here?' she answered equally bluntly.

'It doesn't take much imagination to work out that of course I would be watching my niece ride in her first event on a new horse.'

'I was given to understand that you had an important business meeting today.'

'So I had. This morning.' Alex could feel the suppressed rage waiting to be unleashed. 'That damned child's done it again, hasn't she? More scheming. More futile meddling.' He turned on Alex, his eyes steely with anger. 'But you shouldn't have been fool enough to fall for it.'

'Do you think I'm not telling myself that? But when she said she had got her next hospital date...' Alex suddenly doubted that too. 'Has she?'

'That at least is true,' he said briefly.

'I'm here now. I'll watch Becky ride, then you can rest assured that I shall be off immediately after that. I've no more desire than you to prolong an experience that is obviously totally unwelcome for us both.'

There was silence again while they stared at the fiercely concentrating children urging their ponies along a winding course between poles. Alex wasn't really registering the progress of the race. She doubted that Marcus was either.

'All I wanted was for Becky not to be disappointed by having nobody really involved with Mistral here to see her ride,' she said, smarting with the urge to justify herself.

'And you consider yourself "really involved", do you?' There was cutting sarcasm in his voice. Before she could find an answer to that, he went on, 'For God's sake let's concentrate on the racing. We're attracting unwelcome attention.' He glared at a woman who was eyeing them with interest, making her edge nervously away.

Anna saved the situation by coming back to join them, and Becky's race started. The three people who cared so much for her watched intently now, and so far forgot personal matters as to cheer as wildly as anyone else when Becky came in second—and safe.

'It was worth coming to see that,' Alex said with a defiant look at Marcus. 'But I'm afraid that I must go now. I have other things to do today.'

'You can't leave yet,' Marcus said stonily. 'There'll be a deciding race for the place-winners. Becky could put on an extra spurt and come first. There's no point in being here today if you don't see it through.'

'Oh, yes—do stay and see the presentation of rosettes too,' Anna added with genuinely warm persuasion.

Alex stayed on to see Becky hold on to her second place overall, and felt as though her heart would burst with pride when she saw the tiny figure go forward for her rosette.

'You were terrific!' she told Becky as she hugged her afterwards.

'No, Mistral was.' She patted the horse's neck. 'Aren't you glad you saw her, Alex?'

'I am. But now I must go.'

'But there's tea in the marquee!' Seeing her schemes collapsing, Becky forgot the race and panicked. 'Uncle Marcus, make Alex stay for tea!'

Marcus's stern look brooked no disobedience.

'Alex has other plans for the day. Say goodbye to her now, after which you will go over to the marquee with Anna while I take your guest to her car.'

Becky knew when she had reached the bounds of permissible behaviour. Alex was given a subdued hug, and a whispered, 'I'm sorry, Alex.' Alex knew that the two words were meant to refer to the invitation, not to the child's disappointment that she was leaving.

'Don't worry,' she whispered back. 'But keep your plans for Mistral in future, OK?'

Marcus strode beside her in silence as they went towards the car park.

'This is farcical!' Alex said angrily. 'Do you have to make it look as though you're running me off the premises?'

'Don't be ridiculous. It would be churlish if I didn't see you safely to your car.'

'Doesn't it occur to you that I might prefer that kind of churlishness to a meaningless display of good manners?'

He gave her a cold look. 'I don't happen to be troubling my mind about what you might prefer right now.'

They reached the Mini at last, and when she had unlocked it he put a hand against the driver's door to prevent her getting in.

'I hope you realise how unwise it would be for there to be a repetition of today's happening.'

'Don't worry. There won't be,' Alex said fervently. 'Wild horses wouldn't drag me in this direction again.'

'Never trust wild horses. Two such creatures got us into this regrettable position.' He let go of the door and she slid into the seat, desperate to get away from him.

The engine spluttered once, then refused to show any further sign of life despite Alex's frantic turning of the key. She cursed it under her breath, and tried again.

'There's no point. You'll only finish off the battery,' Marcus said.

'At least we agree about something.' She got out again, locked up the car and set off at a cracking pace along the lane.

'Where do you think you're going?' he asked, his long legs keeping effortlessly up with her.

'To find a garage.'

'There isn't one for miles. And you'll not get anyone who doesn't know you to come out on Saturday afternoon.'

'Then I'll have to walk, won't I?'

He gripped her arm, painfully. 'Stop being such a fool. I'll go and tell Anna what's happening, then I'll bring the car and run you to a chap I know who will probably come out for me.'

'How wonderful to have such power!'

'Cut it out, Alex,' he said sharply. 'Neither of us wants this. Let's just make the best of it until we've got you on the road again.'

He strode off towards the field gate, and once he had gone Alex's anger collapsed and gave way to utter misery. She couldn't bear the way they had spoken to each other all afternoon. And it still wasn't ended. Heaven alone knew how long it would take to get the Mini co-operating again.

Ten gloomy minutes later, the Range Rover drew up beside her.

'You can't just go off and leave two people and a horse to ferry me around,' she said miserably.

'Get in. Of course I'm not just abandoning Anna and Becky. I've arranged for Emma's father to tow Mistral back when they've had tea. They live close to here. It won't take him five minutes to take his lot home and then come back for mine. I'll do the same for him, no doubt, one day.'

Alex sat in silence as they drove along, but at last she said hopelessly, 'I'm sorry about this, Marcus. It was a big mistake, though one made with the most well-intentioned motives.'

'Your motives are what I can't understand,' he said roughly. 'Why pretend to be concerned about Becky? Why not be honest about your feelings?'

'But I do care about Becky!' Alex protested vehemently. 'How could anyone know her and not care about her? Why on earth should you accuse me of that?'

'All moonshine, Alex. You forget that you made no secret of how you felt about Becky on your last night at Chessetts. Yet you still keep up this pretence of affection towards Becky herself. What good will that kind of shallow show do her?'

'What do you mean—I made no secret of my feelings about Becky? And why do you talk of pretence?'

'You said the reason for the break between Elaine and myself still existed. Nothing could be more explicit than that.'

'And so it does. But what is that to do with Becky? It's no fault of hers that you dropped one Leeward like a red-hot poker when you found out who she was, and you're hardly going to deny that you feel exactly the same about me.'

The suddenness with which he jammed on the brakes of the Range Rover would have flung her through the windscreen if she had not been wearing a seatbelt.

'Say that again!' he said, twisting round in his seat to give her the full benefit of the blaze of silver in his eyes. He gripped her arm. 'You said I dropped your sister.'

'Can you deny it?'

'You really think that's what happened?'

'We both know it, don't we?'

His eyes stared fiercely into hers. 'Did Elaine tell you that?'

His intensity was making Alex uncomfortable. 'She was too upset to say anything. She refused to talk about you at all, in fact. But she didn't need to. She was scared stiff of having deceived you about her identity. It was obvious that she lost any appeal she might have had for you the minute she confessed to being a Leeward.'

'That's what you believe?'

'That's what I know,' she said hotly. 'We've got the Atlantic between us and Elaine to prove it.'

'So when you said the reason that separated Elaine and myself still existed to separate you and me, you were referring to the fact that you believed I dropped Elaine because she was a Leeward?'

'How many more times do I have to say what we both know? You can't rewrite history, Marcus.'

'Maybe I can't, as far as you are concerned. But your sister damned well can!'

As quickly as he had halted the Range Rover, he started up the engine and reversed into a gateway to turn and go hurtling back and, with a scream of tyres, turn into a different road.

'Where are you going?' Alex asked, now really frightened.

'Back to Chessetts.'

'You can't do that!' There was panic in her voice.

'Why, Alex?' He sounded almost gleeful. 'Because it would be painful for you? Because you rather liked being there and you don't want to be reminded of that?'

'What's happened to the good manners now?' Alex said ferociously. 'Stop and let me get out if you're going mad, Marcus. I don't want to know.'

'I'll tell you what we're going to do,' he said, his voice full of an energy that was almost manic. 'We're going to telephone that sister of yours.' He slammed the brakes on again. 'You know her number? You've got it on you? Don't say you haven't.'

'You *are* mad!' Alex said, rounding on him wide-eyed.

'I'm nearer to being sane than I have been since I set eyes on that copper head of yours.' There was a glittering, wild look in his eyes.

'You can't seriously talk of phoning my sister and being sane in the same breath.'

'We shall see. Have you got her number? Answer the question, Alex!'

'Yes, but——'

'No buts.' They were hurtling along the road again, with Alex holding grimly on to the edge of her seat.

He had the house key in his hand the second he was out of the car, and dragged Alex in after him, plumping her down on the chair in the hall and pressing the button on the phone that would enable them both to hear the speaker at the other end of the line.

'Get her number,' he ordered.

'We don't know what time it might be over there.'

'Useless delaying tactics, Alex. It's Saturday morning, and there's no earthly reason why your sister shouldn't have a call from you. Go on.'

Stupefied, Alex punched out her sister's number. 'She won't speak to you——' she was saying when the ringing stopped and Elaine's voice announced her number. 'Elaine, it's Alex,' she said, swallowing hard, without a clue what to say next.

Marcus cut in, 'And this is Marcus. How are you, Elaine?'

Elaine's voice was flabbergasted. 'Marcus? Marcus Wakeford? What on earth is going on?'

'Plenty. I want you to do something for me. I want you to tell this sister of yours exactly what happened between us two years ago. Just before you took off for the States, if you need your memory jogged.'

'Marcus—I don't understand what this is all about. Why are you and Alex together?'

'You'll understand, eventually. Right now you don't need to.' Alex was looking fearfully at his determined face and he met her eyes as he went on speaking. 'I want you to tell Alex exactly why you and I parted company. The honest truth. Right, Elaine?'

'This is old hat now, isn't it?' Elaine sounded puzzled but not upset, and Alex would have expected her to be furious—indeed, to have slammed the phone down well before now.

'No. It's highly relevant. Take my word for it.'

'Alex?' Elaine's voice asked.

'I'm here.'

'And I've other urgent business to discuss with her,' Marcus said firmly, 'so please, Elaine—the simple, straightforward facts. I'll start you off. You told me that you were a member of the Leeward family. Take it from there.'

'I don't know why I'm doing this, but here goes,' Elaine's puzzled voice said. 'You laughed. You really did laugh.' Alex's eyes widened as she stared at Marcus. 'Then before we could say anything else the phone rang.' Elaine's voice gathered steam, but at the same time it grew less firm. 'It was the police, calling with news of your brother and his wife... That ghastly accident. You had to go at once, and I waited at your flat. But before you went you said...you said you didn't give a damn for my name, but if I wanted to go on being involved with you I'd have to remember that from now on it wouldn't be just you, but you and your brother's child. Whoever intended taking you seriously would have to be prepared to take on a handicapped child of five as well.' Elaine's voice grew more strained. 'And I sat alone in your flat and eventually had to admit to myself that I didn't want to do that. And that made me realise that I'd been playing games again. I'd made a mess of one marriage. I'd amused myself being mischievous with you. I had to grow up. I've never been so ashamed of myself in my life. I—I told you that in my note.'

Marcus spoke, his voice gentle. 'Well done, Elaine. We're ringing off now, because I need to speak to your sister, but we'll be in touch. And Elaine—no hard feelings, of whatever kind. We're beyond that. Well beyond it.' He pressed the button that disconnected the line, and without pause took Alex's hands in his and pulled her to her feet.

Alex stared at him, her eyes green pools of incredulity. 'Elaine left *you*?' she said.

'Exactly as she told you.'

'And you don't hate me because I'm a Leeward?'

'Do I look as though I hate you?' He was looking at her in a way she had never thought possible. There was tenderness, warmth, everything she could have hoped in the shining grey of his eyes and the understanding gentleness of his expression.

Alex's face became a palette on which the colours of incredulity, hope, tears and joy played. With the utmost tenderness Marcus framed it with his hands.

'Now my question, Alex. Only one. When you spoke of the reason keeping us apart, you didn't mean Becky?

Think hard before you answer, now that the question is in the open and understood.'

'Becky is my idea of a bonus. A bonus on something already ideal,' she said without an instant's hesitation, her eyes brimming with tears.

'Oh, Alex!' He pulled her into his arms. 'Enough of questions. Enough of waiting. All I want is this!'

His first kiss was a tender, loving affirmation of the feelings she had seen on his face. Then something stronger took over and tender affirmation became an exultant madness of kisses. They were both breathless when Marcus broke off to laugh triumphantly down into Alex's glowing, radiant face.

'You don't hate me...' she said, half wonderingly, half laughing.

'Did it *feel* as though I did?' He pressed his face against her hair, crushing her ever more fiercely against him so that she had scarcely enough breath to say teasingly,

'It's going to take some getting used to.'

'Don't worry. I'll give you plenty of practice!'

'I don't mean the kissing. I mean your looking at me as though——' She broke off, blushing, because the words she was about to speak had not yet been spoken between them.

'Oh, Alex!' he chided. 'Don't you know that I have been loving you and hiding it from the moment you blazed your adorable, infuriating, dazzling way into the office at the Mas? Before that, even. From the moment I came across you like Ondine in the stream and thought you were the most beautiful thing I had ever seen. But at first it seemed too ludicrously instant to be believable. Then, when I knew who you were, it seemed utterly impossible. Now——'

'Now it's really true...' she said in such a tone of joyful wonder that the lips that had just spoken were claimed once more by his.

'We have still to tell my parents,' she said at last.

'They'll take one look at your face and believe every word you say. They'll see your happiness and rejoice in it.'

'And Elaine.'

'Elaine is happily married. I shall be even more happily married. Where's the problem in that?'

'You really meant it when you said there were no more hard feelings?'

'My love, Elaine was fun and attractive, but she was never a millionth part of what you have become in my life. You're the real, the lasting thing. The bitterness I felt for her was because simply by being your sister she seemed to be keeping us apart, colouring your attitudes, spoiling our lives. But now that's all over. She's the sister of the girl who loves me!'

Alex clasped her arms more tightly round his neck and said, 'If you tell me that this isn't paradise I shan't believe you.'

There was the sound of a vehicle drawing up outside the house. They went to the door, arms round each other.

A small figure got awkwardly out of the car, not seeing them, and stood a little forlornly on the drive.

'Can we make room for one small angel with us in this paradise of ours?' Marcus asked, smiling.

And together they went out to light up Becky's world.

4 FREE

Romances and 2 FREE gifts just for you!

You can enjoy all the heartwarming emotion of true love for FREE! Discover the heartbreak and happiness, the emotion and the tenderness of the modern relationships in Mills & Boon Romances.

We'll send you 4 Romances as a special offer from Mills & Boon Reader Service, along with the opportunity to have 6 captivating new Romances delivered to your door each month.

Claim your FREE books and gifts overleaf...

An irresistible offer from Mills & Boon

Become a regular reader of Romances with Mills & Boon Reader Service and we'll welcome you with 4 books, a CUDDLY TEDDY and a special MYSTERY GIFT all absolutely FREE.

And then look forward to receiving 6 brand new Romances each month, delivered to your door hot off the presses, postage and packing FREE! Plus our free Newsletter featuring author news, competitions, special offers and much more.

This invitation comes with no strings attached. You may cancel or suspend your subscription at any time, and still keep your free books and gifts.

It's so easy. Send no money now. Simply fill in the coupon below and post it to -
Reader Service, FREEPOST, PO Box 236, Croydon, Surrey CR9 9EL.

— — — — — **NO STAMP REQUIRED** — — — — —

Free Books Coupon

Yes! Please rush me 4 FREE Romances and 2 FREE gifts! Please also reserve me a Reader Service subscription. If I decide to subscribe I can look forward to receiving 6 brand new Romances for just £11.40 each month, postage and packing FREE. If I decide not to subscribe I shall write to you within 10 days - I can keep the free books and gifts whatever I choose. I may cancel or suspend my subscription at any time. I am over 18 years of age.

Ms/Mrs/Miss/Mr _____ EP71R

Address _____

_____

Postcode _____ Signature _____

HEARTS OF FIRE

By Miranda Lee

HEARTS OF FIRE by Miranda Lee is a totally compelling six-part saga set in Australia's glamorous but cut-throat world of gem dealing.

Discover the passion, scandal, sin and finally the hope that exists between two fabulously rich families. You'll be hooked from the very first page…

Each of the six novels in this series features a gripping romance. And the first title **SEDUCTION AND SACRIFICE** can be yours absolutely FREE! You can also reserve the remaining five novels in this exciting series from Reader Service, delivered to your door for £2.50 each. And remember postage and packing is FREE!

MILLS & BOON READER SERVICE, FREEPOST, P.O. BOX 236, CROYDON CR9 9EL. TEL: 081-684 2141

- -

YES! Please send me my FREE book (part 1 in the Hearts of Fire series) and reserve me a subscription for the remaining 5 books in the series. I understand that you will send me one book each month and invoice me £2.50 each month.

NO STAMP NEEDED

MILLS & BOON READER SERVICE, FREEPOST, P.O. BOX 236, CROYDON CR9 9EL. TEL: 081-684 2141

Ms/Mrs/Miss/Mr: _____ EPHOF

Address _____

_____

_____

Postcode _____